On the rare occasion Finn had allowed the memory of Georgie to flow unfettered through his mind, she either sat at the bar, exuding confidence and vibrancy and dazzling him with flirty banter and smoldering smiles, or lay sprawled across his bed as morning dawned, looking flushed and tousled and sleepily sexy.

Now, with the bombshell she'd just dropped, he couldn't think at all.

His mind had gone blank. His pulse was thundering and a cold sweat had broken out all over his skin. His vision was blurred. The room seemed to be spinning.

"What?" he said roughly, his voice sounding as if it came from far, far away while the disorientation intensified.

"You, well, *we* have a son," she said. "Josh. He's six months old."

Lucy King

THE SECRETS SHE MUST TELL

HARLEQUIN®
PRESENTS®

Recycling programs
for this product may
not exist in your area.

ISBN-13: 978-1-335-40376-6

The Secrets She Must Tell

Harlequin Enterprises ULC
22 Adelaide St. West, 40th Floor
Toronto, Ontario M5H 4E3, Canada
www.Harlequin.com

Printed in U.S.A.

Lucy King spent her adolescence lost in the glamorous and exciting world of Harlequin when she really ought to have been paying attention to her teachers. But as she couldn't live in a dream world forever, she eventually acquired a degree in languages and an eclectic collection of jobs. After a decade in southwest Spain, Lucy now lives with her young family in Wiltshire, England. When not writing or trying to think up new and innovative things to do with mince, she spends her time reading, failing to finish cryptic crosswords and dreaming of the golden beaches of Andalucia.

Books by Lucy King

Harlequin Presents

Passion in Paradise

A Scandal Made in London

Other books by Lucy King

The Couple Behind the Headlines
One More Sleepless Night
The Reunion Lie
One Night with Her Ex
The Best Man for the Job
The Party Starts at Midnight

Visit the Author Profile page
at Harlequin.com for more titles.

PROLOGUE

SHE COULDN'T TAKE her eyes off him.

Sitting on the crimson velvet banquette that curved around a table upon which sat a bottle of bubbles chilling in a bucket, Georgie Wallace took a sip of champagne and felt it fizz down her throat to join the unfamiliar buzzing in her stomach.

Her pulse thudded in time to the beat of the sultry music drifting over from the dance floor. The blood pounding through her veins was thick and hot. This pull, this dizzying breathlessness, this inability to concentrate on the conversation going on around her had never happened to her before.

But then, she'd never seen anyone quite like *him* before either.

She'd noticed him the moment he'd entered the room what felt like an eternity ago but could only have been a matter of seconds. One minute she'd been laughing at something one of her friends had said, the next the air had started vibrating with a strange sort of electric tension that had sizzled straight through her, igniting her nerve-endings and robbing her of all coherent thought. Her gaze had located the source of it with the precision of a heat-seeking missile, and the impact of seeing him had dealt a blow to her senses from which she'd yet to recover.

Now he was striding across the floor away from her, dominating the space as if he owned it, all towering height, confident authority and purposeful intent. Anyone in his way instinctively stepped out of it. No one appeared inclined to inform him of the club's no-jeans policy.

'Magnificent,' Georgie murmured to herself, watching transfixed as he slid onto a stool at the far end of the busy bar and summoned the bartender with nothing more than a barely perceptible lift of his head.

That was what he was.

In command.

Compelling.

And clearly in need of a drink, if the way he knocked back the one that appeared in front of him was anything to go by.

'Huh?' said Carla, her oldest and best friend, who was sitting beside her and who she could see out of the corner of her eye was bopping to the music while plucking the bottle from the bucket to refill her glass.

'The guy at the bar,' Georgie said, unable to wrench her gaze away.

'Which one?'

Wasn't it obvious? 'Far left. Dark hair in need of a cut, checked shirt.'

'Big and broad with his sleeves pushed up?'

'That's him.'

Carla replaced the bottle in the bucket and sat back. 'A bit dishevelled for my liking,' she said after a moment's consideration. 'Nice back, though. Good shoulders.'

'Very.' With muscles clearly visible beneath the cotton that stretched across them, they were possibly the finest set of shoulders Georgie had ever seen.

'Did you get a look at his face?'

'Not properly.' Just a tantalising glimpse of a strong masculine jaw and straight nose as he'd stridden past her.

'It would be helpful if he shifted round a bit more.'

'True,' Georgie said with an assessing tilt of her head. 'But even if he did, he'd still be too far away to make out the details.'

'Shame.'

It was indeed, because just imagine if his face matched up to the promise of his body. He'd be breathtakingly gorgeous and that was something she wouldn't mind taking a good, long look at.

But, intriguingly, what was equally as arresting as his physique on the move was his stillness and his containment as he sat alone at the bar. Now furnished with another drink, which he was taking more slowly than the last, he seemed to be utterly lost in thought, an island of immobility in a sea of activity, his bleak sobriety a sharp contrast to the hedonistic atmosphere of the club, and oddly desolate.

Who was he?

What was he doing here?

And would he like some company?

At *that* distantly familiar thought, Georgie inwardly stilled, her heart skipping a beat before racing.

Oooh, how *interesting*.

Once upon a time, as an out-of-control teenager desperate for parental attention and discipline, she hadn't thought twice about approaching good-looking men in bars for a spot of light flirting or dirty dancing, and she'd been extremely good at it.

But ever since she'd come to the distressing realisation at the age of sixteen that if she wanted boundaries she'd have to set them for herself, she'd given up that sort of reckless, impulsive behaviour and had knuckled down to the serious business of adulting. With a love of rules that had been missing from her upbringing, she'd pursued a career in law—much to the horror of her hippie parents—and had slowly built the structure she craved into her life.

She'd had dates, of course, relationships even, but they were casual affairs with guys at college or, later, with men she generally met at friends' dinner parties, men she already faintly knew instead of random strangers picked up in bars.

And, while she'd liked and respected and fancied all of them, none had made her heart race particularly fast. Her last relationship—six months with a perfectly nice but ultimately unexciting banker—had fizzled out over a year ago and she'd neither lamented its demise nor been on the lookout for another.

For the last twelve months, in fact, she'd become so engrossed in the job she loved, so determined to get the promotion she'd been after, that she hadn't given the opposite sex a moment's consideration. She hadn't wanted the distraction. She hadn't needed the hassle.

Tonight, however, with her promotion in the bag and her foot easing off the accelerator a fraction, it appeared she wouldn't mind some of both.

'Good *song*,' Carla said in response to a shift in the music as she bopped about on the seat a bit more energetically. 'Want to dance?'

Not particularly.

In fact, Georgie wanted something quite different. Because, while hitting the dance floor with her friends and forgetting all about the brooding hunk at the bar would be by far the safest, most sensible option, she didn't *want* to forget about him. And for once she didn't *want* to be sensible. She wanted to meet him. Talk to him. Flirt with him. She wanted to give in to the scorching heat and the dizzying lust rushing through her and see where they took her.

She couldn't remember the last time she'd experienced such an intense and immediate attraction, or felt so alive. She hadn't realised how much she'd missed the heady thrill of sexual excitement, how long she'd been treading water. Besides, it was her birthday. If she couldn't let her hair down tonight of all nights, when could she?

'Maybe later,' she said, her stomach tightening and her pulse racing at the thought of what could happen if she went for it.

Beside her, Carla stilled, her eyes wide. 'Oh? But you usually love dancing.'

'I think I might go over and see if I can't cheer him up instead.'

There was a moment of stunned silence, and then an incredulous, 'Seriously?'

'Why not?'

'Because he does *not* look like the sort of suave, sophisticated professional you usually go for these days. He looks…untamed.'

'I know.' And that was the attraction.

'Are you certain?'

'Yup.' Ish. Her chatting up skills were a bit rusty, and not only might he not be in the mood for company, he might also be spoken for. But what was the worst that could happen? If she crashed and burned, she could always give a nonchalant shrug and leave. If, on the other hand, she didn't, and the attraction she was experiencing turned out to be mutual… well…the outcome could be explosive.

'I thought you'd given up doing that sort of thing.'

'It's only conversation,' she said while thinking, Well, maybe. To start with, at least.

'Sure it is,' said Carla with a wry grin that Georgie couldn't help returning as she put down her glass and got to her feet, her stomach churning with nervous excitement.

'Wish me luck.'

'Good luck. Not that you ever needed it. One thing, though…'

'What?'

'Just in case it *isn't* only conversation and you leave before we're back from the dance floor, message me his name and a photo, and call me in the morning.'

Oblivious to the energy and buzz surrounding him, Finn Calvert stared unseeingly into his drink, his usually ordered thoughts a jumble, his legendary focus blitzed.

Twelve months. Eighteen at most. That was how long his father had left.

Details of the phone call he'd received an hour ago, which had ripped him apart and shattered his world, ricocheted around his head.

Four weeks ago, unbeknownst to him, his father had gone to his doctor complaining of a prolonged cough and shortness of breath. Subsequent tests had revealed lung cancer. Metastasised. Incurable.

Devastating.

Ever since his mother's death when he was young his father had been his only family. He'd been the one who'd brought him up and who'd fished him out of the trouble he'd got into as an angry teenager.

When, at eighteen, Finn had announced he wanted to buy the bar where he'd been working and which was up for sale, his father had been his initial investor. Over the years he'd subsequently proved a solid sounding board and his staunchest supporter, and the bond they shared was deep and unassailable.

Now he was dying, and there wasn't a thing he— Finn—with all his wealth and influence, success and power, could do about it.

His jaw clenched and his fingers tightened around the glass as he fought back a hot surge of emotion, a tangle of helplessness, injustice and rage. Why had his father waited so long before seeing his GP? Why hadn't ever he said anything about not feeling well?

And how had *he* not noticed that anything had been wrong? His father could be guarded at times and had practically invented the stiff upper lip, but that was no excuse. Nor was the acquisition of a hugely grand yet derelict Parisian hotel, the renovation of which had become so complex that Finn had barely had a moment's thought for anything else. He should have made time. He should have visited his father more often. Then he might have seen that something wasn't right.

But he hadn't and now it was too late, and the guilt and the regret were crucifying him in a way that, contrary to his hopes, alcohol was doing nothing to dull. All he wanted from the whisky he was drinking was oblivion. Just for tonight. There'd be time for stoicism and practicality in the morning. But the whisky might as well have been water because the pain was as excoriating as it had been an hour ago and his chest still felt as if it were caught in an ever-tightening vice.

By coming here he'd chosen the wrong place, he thought, downing the remainder of his drink and feeling the burn momentarily scythe through the turmoil. It was convenient, certainly, but it was too loud, too damn full of fun and laughter. He ought to leave and go in search of a darker, quieter, harder bar, one where he could sit on his own in the shadows and the alcohol would flow without question.

And he ought to leave now.

'Hi.'

The soft voice came from his right, puncturing the fog swirling around in his head and freezing him mid-move. The sexy, feminine timbre of it hit him low in the gut and wound through him from there, heating the blood suddenly rushing through his veins and reigniting sensation everywhere.

Automatically, Finn lifted his head and turned it in her direction. She was standing a foot from him, enveloping him with an intoxicating combination of heat and scent, confidence and vibrancy. His gaze locked onto hers, and in that instant the overall impression he had of dark, tousled hair, dazzling smile and a short black sequinned dress was pulverised by a punch of lust so strong it nearly knocked him off his stool.

Lost in the soft brown depths of her eyes and unable to look away, he felt his pulse slow right down. The noise and activity of the club faded. His surroundings disappeared. His head emptied of everything but a strange sense of recognition.

Which was absurd, he told himself, getting a grip and blinking to snap the connection. His foundations had been rocked. His defences were weak. Recognition? No way. They didn't know each other.

But they could.

They could get to know each other *very* well.

Because the intense attraction that had hit him like the blow of a hammer was not one-sided, he realised as he let his gaze drift over her in a leisurely assessment. She felt it too. Quite apart from the fact that she'd been the one to approach him, he could see it in the dilation of her pupils and the rapid rise and fall of her chest. In the flush on her cheeks and the accelerated flutter of the pulse at the base of her neck. He could hear it in the hitch of her breath and feel it in the way she was now very slightly leaning towards him.

And it occurred to him then that perhaps there were other ways to achieve the mindlessness he craved. Perhaps a night of hot sex and dizzying pleasure would succeed where alcohol had failed. Just the thought of it was pushing aside his father's devastating diagnosis and his own reaction to it. Imagine the reality. If he switched his focus and put his mind to it he wouldn't even have to imagine.

'Hello,' he said, giving her a slow smile that had

felled many a woman over the years and was clearly no less effective tonight, if the sparkle that appeared in her eyes was anything to go by.

'Would you mind if I joined you?'

'I can't think of anything I'd like more.'

CHAPTER ONE

Fifteen months later

STILL NO NEWS.

Oblivious to the faint thud of music coming from the club below, Finn tossed his phone onto his desk and stalked to the window, frustration boiling through him as he stared out through the Georgian sash window into the dark London night.

It had been two months since he'd found the adoption certificate amongst the papers left behind by the man he'd always considered to be his father, and he was no closer to discovering the truth surrounding his birth now than he had been the moment he'd figured out what he was holding and his life, already shattered by grief, had blown fully apart. The only people who could shed any light on anything were no longer around to ask, and the investigation agency he'd hired—allegedly one of the best in the country— had hit a dead end with every lead.

The paralysis was driving him demented. All he

wanted was answers. All he needed was clarity. He'd
thought the sorrow and emptiness that had consumed
him in the days following his father's—no, *Jim's*—
death and the realisation that he was now all alone
in the world had been harrowing, but at least there'd
been a feeling of closure. At least there'd been a logi-
cal, if agonising, process to get through.

Now there was nothing but chaos. Where order
and certainty had once ruled Finn's world, confusion
and doubt now reigned. He no longer knew what to
believe; facts he'd never once had cause to examine
now tormented him day and night. Who was he?
Where did he come from?

The questions that spun around his head and left
scorching trails of betrayal in their wake were many
and relentless. Why had he been adopted? Where and
who was his real family? Had he been abandoned?
How had he ended up where he had?

And, most crushingly, why had he never been
told the truth? There'd been eleven thousand opportunities to explain the circumstances surrounding
his adoption, give or take a day or two, and eleven
thousand opportunities missed. Why keep it a secret?
His father, the man he'd so admired and looked up
to, who'd circled the wagons when his mother had
died and to whom he'd turned for advice and support
back in the early days of his business, had become a
stranger overnight.

As a result Finn had no idea how much of his
thirty-one years on the planet had been genuine and

how much hadn't. In the absence of fact, his previously staid imagination ran riot. In the darkest moments, when he couldn't sleep and prowled around his penthouse apartment unable to stop the constant churning of his mind, he found himself revisiting the circumstances of his mother's death. He'd only been ten when she'd stepped out into a road and been hit by a bus. The driver had sworn she'd seen him coming, had even looked him straight in the eye, but why would she have done it deliberately, a pale-faced, tight-jawed Jim had immediately countered, when she'd had no reason to take her own life and everything to live for?

The coroner had ruled her death an accident and Jim had always unflinchingly maintained this verdict, but in the cool, calm quiet of the early hours of the past couple of weeks the doubts had crept into Finn's head and taken root. Jim had lied to him about his birth, had lied to him his entire life, and now he couldn't help thinking, what if he'd been lying about that too? What if his mother's death *hadn't* been an accident? What if every time she looked at him, her *adopted* son, she was reminded of what she'd never been able to create for herself? What if that had finally become too much to bear? What if she'd deliberately stepped in front of that bus because of him, because in some way he'd failed her, because he'd behaved too badly or somehow hadn't been a good enough son?

If he'd been able to think logically, rationally, he

might have seen this extrapolation for the unlikelihood it was, but logic and reason were long gone. His identity, his history, his entire belief system had been decimated and he didn't know what to think or who to trust any more. He couldn't even trust himself. He'd been taken for a fool and deceived his whole life, yet had never suspected a thing. The instincts he'd always considered rock solid and uncannily reliable were clearly worthless, and as a result his ruthlessly efficient decision-making ability had vanished. His concentration was shot and his attention to detail was history. His usually long fuse was now microscopically short, and he was snapping and snarling at anyone who had the misfortune to cross his path.

He neither recognised nor liked the man he'd become, a man who no longer knew his place in a world he'd always dominated, but there didn't seem to be a damn thing he could do about it. The armour he'd taken for granted had been brutally stripped away and he was all at sea, unanchored and rudderless, and it was hell.

'Boss?'

Shaking free of his tumultuous thoughts, Finn turned from the window to see the club's doorman standing in the doorway.

'Yes?' he all but growled.

Bob, built like a tank and in possession of an attitude to match, didn't even flinch. 'There's someone looking for you.'

'Who?'

'No idea. But she's outside, asking if anyone knows you.'

'She?'

'Brunette. Mid-to-late twenties, I'd say. Slim. Could be stunning if she tried. Not really dressed for partying. She's saying she met you in the bar the October before last. She sounds like a fruitcake if you ask me, but I thought you should know in case she turns out to be a crazy stalker or something.'

Finn's brows snapped together. 'CCTV?'

'Sure.'

The doorman pulled a device from the inside of his jacket and hit a couple of buttons. 'There she is,' he said, pointing at a figure on the screen.

Finn took the device, examined the live feed and froze, his entire body clenching with recognition and an unwelcome punch of heat.

Georgie.

Once met, never entirely forgotten, much to his irritation.

If he chose to, he could recall the night they'd spent together as clearly as if it had been yesterday. The heated looks they'd exchanged at the bar, the heavily laden conversation, the bizarrely intense connection… The chemistry between them had been incredible. The sex had been hot and wild, the best he'd ever had. Over and over again that night she'd given him the oblivion he'd craved, and for a brief mad moment as dawn had broken he'd been tempted to ask for her number before remembering that they'd agreed to one uncomplicated night only, and, in his case, why that was. He'd had enough on his plate with Jim's illness. He'd been in no way looking for anything more. But that hadn't stopped her invading his dreams and giving him uncomfortably sleepless nights for weeks afterwards.

'What does she want?' he asked, ignoring the heat and handing the device back with an odd sort of reluctance.

'She won't say. Just keeps flashing around this photo of you on her phone.'

The same photo she'd taken outside his club, *just in case*, she'd said with a foxy smile that had thumped him square in the chest? Had to be. She wouldn't have found one anywhere else. Despite owning a company whose portfolio boasted seven-star hotels, top-end bars and clubs, and restaurants with six-month waiting lists, he rarely appeared in the media. He didn't need to; the firm that dealt with his PR was outstanding.

'What would you like me to do?'

Good question, thought Finn, shoving his hands in his pockets as he searched for the answer that not so long ago would have come to him instantly. If Georgie had come looking for him before his entire life had been turned upside down he'd have wondered if perhaps she'd been having as much trouble forgetting him as he had her, and whether she might be up for a repeat performance.

But now he didn't know what to think and because

he didn't, because his behaviour was currently so unpredictable, he ought to have her sent on her way and put her out of his mind. Besides, he didn't need to know why she was here. They were done months ago and the last thing he wanted was potentially even more chaos and complication.

And yet for some unfathomable reason, despite his better judgement, he *wanted* to know why she was looking for him, now, after all this time. It intrigued him, shifted his focus and gave him a welcome respite from the turmoil. Frankly, her reason for showing up here couldn't be any more destructive than anything else that had happened to him over the last couple of months, could it? 'Send her up.'

With a heavy heart, Georgie locked her phone and stuck it back in her bag, weariness and despondency washing over her in a great, drowning wave. Coming to the club where she and Finn had met all those months ago had been a long shot, but she hadn't known where else to try.

She'd spent two days trying to track him down with nothing to go on except his first name and a photo. Unsurprisingly, the internet had yielded nothing. The records held by the hotel in which they'd spent the night were data protected, and her enquiries here had met with blank stares and stony silence.

Which meant she was all out of options and back at square one, she thought, anxiety churning around in her gut as the hopelessness of her situation hit her all over again. She had no job, little money and home was, for the moment, a tiny, damp bedsit in a crime-ridden part of London. Because of what had happened, she was unemployable. Her prospects were nil. Her confidence had hit rock bottom and her judgement was unreliable. How she was going to manage going forward she had no idea.

Digging deep to stave off the relentless despair, Georgie turned to leave, only to freeze when she heard a brusque, 'Stop.'

She swung round, her heart banging against her ribs, to see the man with the muscles and the unpromising attitude, he of the stony silence and blank stare, bearing down on her.

'Don't worry, I'm going,' she said, lifting her hands and backing off as he came to a halt in front of her.

'Wait.'

She blinked. 'What?'

'The man you're looking for,' he said curtly. 'He's upstairs.'

At the unexpected information, Georgie's stomach gave a great lurch and her pulse leapt. 'Really?' she said, glancing up and seeing nothing but dark windows and an absence of movement.

'Follow me.'

He turned smartly on his heel and, for a moment, she dithered. Was it true? Could she really have found him at last? On the other hand, how likely was it that Finn was indeed up there? Why would he be? What if Muscles was part of some dastardly trafficking scheme or something and taking her to a place from which she wouldn't return?

No.

Ridiculous. That was what she was being. Utterly ridiculous. She was in no danger. She needed to banish the wreck she was these days, beat back the paranoia and channel the fearless Georgie of the October fifteen months ago, who hadn't hesitated to go for what she wanted and watch out anyone who got in her way. The old her was in there somewhere. She had to be.

Gritting her teeth, Georgie determinedly shook off the frightening darkness that was gathering at the edges of her mind in an all too familiar way and the memory of the confusing, terrifying thoughts that had consumed her for much of the last six months, and set off in the doorman's wake. She stepped through the door and into the club, and was immediately hit by a wall of noise, a burst of heat, and a deluge of memories that had her momentarily stopping in her tracks with their vividness.

There was the bar where she'd walked up to Finn and asked if she could join him, she thought, recalling the desire that had swept through her when she'd looked at him and realised he was as breathtakingly gorgeous as she'd hoped. Where he'd given her that devastatingly wicked smile and she'd known in that instant that they'd be leaving together. Where they'd sat close and flirted, their gazes locked, their bodies communicating on an entirely different level, their off-the-charts chemistry sizzling and soaring until they hadn't been able to take any more.

When she'd breathed into his ear that she wanted to leave—with him—he'd taken her hand and led her out of the club with flatteringly indecent speed. He'd pulled her into a dark doorway and kissed her until her knees went weak and her stomach dissolved into a puddle of lust. He'd then taken her back to his hotel room where they'd spent hours burning up the sheets of his bed before parting in the morning with no promises and no regrets.

It had been everything she'd been hoping for.

It had been perfect.

And then, a while later, not so perfect.

With a sigh, Georgie let go of the memories, and resumed her progress across the room, aware of the curious glances she was attracting, which were hardly surprising, since her appearance gave a whole new meaning to the phrase 'dressing down'. She hadn't dressed up for this meeting. She hadn't dressed up for anything in a long time. Would her zest for life, her energy, her libido, ever come back? Would *she* ever wholly come back? Who knew?

As she followed the doorman up the stairs at the back of the club her heart began to thump, not with excitement, as it had the last time she'd been here, but with nerves. How was this going to go? She didn't have a clue. On one level she was sure that seeking Finn out was the right—the only—thing to do. Yet, on another, she didn't know him, she didn't know how he was going to react, and therefore the outcome was scarily unpredictable.

At the top of two flights of stairs Muscles rapped on a door and opened it. He stood to one side and gestured for her to go in. Georgie took a deep breath in through her nose that she let out slowly through her mouth, and, on legs that felt like jelly, stepped forwards.

And there he was. Standing at the window in the shadows with his back to her, the same broad, muscled back she'd raked her nails down while gasping his name and writhing with pleasure.

The door closed behind her. Finn turned and her breath left her lungs. She'd forgotten just how attractive he was. How breathtaking the impact of his indigo gaze on her could be. The intensity of his focus sent an unexpected bolt of heat shooting through her that for the briefest of moments sliced through the icy numbness she'd lived with for what felt like for ever and made her wish she had the energy to care about the whole make-up-hair-clothes thing.

As the seconds stretched and the silence throbbed she dragged her gaze from his and ran it over the rest of him. He looked harder than she remembered, as if life had knocked him about a bit. Less forgiving too, which perhaps didn't bode well for this meeting. Possibly even a bit wary about why she was turning up out of the blue like this. None the less compelling, though. None the less in command as he stood there utterly still, utterly in control, his feet apart and his hands in his pockets. And if he seemed bigger and broader than she remembered...well, maybe that was because she'd shrunk.

She lifted her eyes back up to his and she thought she saw a flicker of heat, of shock, in the depths of his. But it disappeared before she could work out if she was right, and whatever he'd been thinking was now hidden behind a mask of neutrality. She couldn't gauge how he felt about her being here. Or if he felt anything at all, for that matter. Not that he had any reason to. What they'd had had been a mutually agreed one-night stand, nothing more. She'd hardly expected the same laid-back, full-on seduction she'd been on the receiving end of when she'd initially approached him all those months ago. She wasn't expecting anything. Hoping for, yes, but expecting, no.

'Hello,' she said hoarsely, her heart pounding and her mouth dry. 'So you probably don't remember me, but—'

'I remember you.'

'Good,' she said with a shaky attempt at a smile. That made things slightly easier. At least she didn't have to first explain how they knew each other. 'How have you been?'

A shadow flitted across his expression. 'Fine. You?'

Not quite so fine, actually, although there was no way she was telling him how not fine she'd been. She had far too much to lose. 'Couldn't be better.'

'I'm delighted to hear it.'

'I can't believe I found you.'

'How hard have you been trying?'

'Very. I didn't have much to go on. Just your first name and the photo I took when we left here that night.'

He gave the briefest of nods. 'Just in case.'

'It seemed sensible.'

'You kept it.'

'As a memento.' Which, in hindsight, was deeply ironic when she'd ended up with a memento of a totally different kind. 'Anyway, I remembered that you looked comfortable at the bar. You didn't pay the bill. I wondered if you had a tab and, if you did, whether you might be a regular. Now I know differently.' She glanced around the softly lit space that contained a mahogany desk, a couple of chairs and sage green walls lined with books. 'Do you manage the club downstairs?'

'I own it.'

Right. That made sense. He'd said he worked in hospitality and he hadn't struck her as the type to take orders. 'No wonder no one threw you out for wearing jeans.'

His dark brows snapped together in a deep frown. 'What?'

'Nothing.'

'As fascinating as this trip down memory lane is, Georgie, I'm busy. So get to the point. What are you doing here? What do you want?'

He was right. The time for dithering was over. Finn had a right to know and she badly needed any support he might be prepared to offer. She stuck her hands into the back pockets of her jeans to hide the trembling and took a deep breath. 'Well, the thing is, you…we…well, basically, Finn, our one-night stand left me pregnant and as a result you have a son.'

CHAPTER TWO

WHEN FINN HAD instructed Bob to send Georgie up he hadn't given much thought to what he was expecting with regards to her appearance. On the rare occasion he'd allowed the memory of her to flow unfettered through his mind, she either sat at the bar, exuding confidence and vibrancy and dazzling him with flirty banter and smouldering smiles, or lay sprawled across his bed as morning dawned, looking flushed and tousled and sleepily sexy.

He barely recognised the on-edge, wary version standing in front of him. Her dark hair was scraped back from a face that was ghostly pale. Her eyes were dull and her cheeks hollow. Her clothes were hanging off her. Above the neckline of her white T-shirt, her collarbones stuck out, and her jeans hung loose on her hips despite her belt being tightly buckled. It was as if someone had switched off her light, and once he'd got over his shock he'd found himself wondering what had happened to her.

Now, with the bombshell she'd just dropped, he

couldn't think at all. His mind had gone blank. His pulse was thundering and a cold sweat had broken out all over his skin. His vision was blurred. The room seemed to be spinning.

'What?' he said roughly, his voice sounding as if it came from far, far away while the disorientation intensified.

'You, well, *we*, have a son,' she said. 'Josh. He's six months old.'

A son.

Josh.

Six months old.

The words flew through the air, bulldozing a path through the chaos and hitting his brain like bullets, where they pulverised the fog and cleared the way for indisputable logic and instinctive denial.

A baby?

His baby?

It was impossible.

Or at the very least improbable.

'We can't,' he said thickly, grappling for some kind of hold on this.

'We can. We do.'

'You said you were on the pill.'

'I was.'

'So what happened?'

'I don't know,' she said with a slight frown. 'I might have been sick. Or on antibiotics. I don't remember.'

Disbelief barrelled through him. 'You don't remember?'

'No.'

How could she be so cool, so calm? Could she possibly have done it deliberately? At the thought his blood chilled and his gut churned. 'How convenient.'

Her eyes narrowed. 'What are you suggesting?'

'What do you think?'

Her chin came up. 'Believe me, I did *not* plan it. I did not plan *any* of it.'

'What makes you think he's mine?'

'You're the only person I slept with at the time. The last person I slept with actually.'

'Do you expect me to believe that simply because you say so?'

'Well, yes. But it doesn't matter. I have photos,' she said, twisting slightly to rummage around in her bag before extracting her phone and fiddling with it for a moment. 'Here.' She walked over to him and held out the device. 'Take a look. Swipe left. There are lots.'

For a moment Finn stared at the phone as if it were a live grenade. His heart hammered against his ribs. He went hot, then cold. He wanted to look. He didn't want to look. He didn't know what he wanted, but it didn't seem to matter because, with a hand that wasn't entirely steady, he was reaching for the phone anyway and lowering his gaze, and one glance at the screen was enough to detonate what remained of an already shattered life. Because the baby in the photo, with his shock of thick, dark hair, laughing blue eyes, and rosy, chubby cheeks was the spitting image of him at a similar age.

The blow of recognition winded him so hard he couldn't breathe. The floor tipped beneath his feet and his knees nearly gave way. But somehow he remained upright and somehow he managed to blindly swipe through the pictures that followed, the overwhelming sense of familiarity intensifying with every passing second.

The truth of the child's parentage was undeniable.

Which meant that he was a father.

A violent rush of emotion rocked though him then, tangling up with the issues surrounding his own parentage and his feelings about Jim and Alice, which he couldn't even *begin* to unravel. And quite suddenly, out of the hot, bubbling chaos roared a protective instinct he didn't know he had and a clamouring primitive need to claim what was his above all else.

He could forget for now that Georgie had kept the existence of this child from him. He could ignore the myriad questions bombarding his head, adding to the confusion and turmoil. There'd be time for explanations and answers and analysis later. Right now he wanted—no, *needed*—to see his son.

'Where is he?' he said, handing her phone back and knowing the images on it would remain imprinted on his memory for ever.

'With a friend.'

'Take me to him.'

She stared at him for a moment, her eyebrows shooting up. 'Now?'

'I've missed all six months of my son's life,' he said, his jaw tightening and his tone chilly as he thought briefly of how much she'd denied him even if he didn't yet understand it. 'I don't intend to miss a moment longer. So yes, Georgie. Now.'

In an ideal world, Georgie would have chosen to introduce Finn to his son on neutral territory, such as a park or a café, or, really, anywhere other than the dingy bedsit she now called home. However, she hadn't thought it wise to suggest they wait until morning. Once he'd recovered from the shock, Finn's stunned disbelief had very obviously turned to simmering anger, and why would she want to provoke that?

Sitting in the passenger seat of the top-of-the-range car that he was driving through the dark streets of the city and feeling the tension still radiating off him in great waves, Georgie could understand his animosity and resentment. From his point of view, she'd deliberately kept her pregnancy and his son from him. She'd denied him key moments in Josh's life. He didn't know that she hadn't even realised she'd been pregnant until she'd given birth. He didn't know that, subsequently caught in the terrifying grip of post-partum psychosis, she hadn't had the capacity to track him down. Nor did he know that as soon as she'd recov-

ered enough to be able to make a choice about what
to do next, she'd gone about rectifying that.

Nevertheless, despite Finn's stony silence and
tightly leashed displeasure, she was glad she'd managed to find him, and unbelievably relieved that he
appeared to want to be involved. His reaction to her
blurted revelation could have gone either way. They
barely knew each other. When they'd originally met
it had been all about the sex. Neither had been looking for an in-depth character analysis of the other
and, while she had felt an odd sense of connection,
conversation had been sparse. So, upon hearing
about Josh, Finn could easily have simply handed
her phone back, told her he wasn't interested and
thrown her out. But he hadn't, and for that she was
inordinately grateful.

She was also more than a little nervous, she had
to admit as she laced her fingers tightly in her lap
while her stomach began to churn. At the moment
he looked to be too busy absorbing the shock of fatherhood to question why it had taken her so long
to contact him, but there'd come a point when he'd
ask. And when he did, what would she say? He didn't
seem the sort to be satisfied with a vague 'it's been a
busy time' kind of explanation, yet she'd never told
anyone the full extent of what she'd been through,
not even Carla.

So should she tell him? As Josh's father, he deserved to know the whole unvarnished story, and as
part of her recovery it had been recommended she

share it. But if she did, what would he think? What would he do? There were so many possible outcomes to this thing she'd set in motion, she thought, her stomach knotting as she stared out into the damp night. Some she could only hope for, some she dreaded, some remained unknown.

But one thing *was* certain.

While she couldn't avoid telling Finn the truth for ever, she could at least put it off until he actually asked. Maybe even beyond that. She didn't have to share it all *now*. And so, until the moment of reckoning came, until she had no option but to confess all and hope for the best, she was saying nothing.

If Finn had been asked to describe the route he'd just driven or name the neighbourhood in which he now found himself he'd have drawn a blank. The moment he'd registered the fact that he was on his way to meet his son, everything had become a blur, a great maelstrom of emotions and thoughts that he could barely absorb, let alone process. He'd had to shut down in order to be able to concentrate on driving and that was how he'd remained during the entire half-hour journey.

Now, however, as he stood in a room that was smaller than his en-suite bathroom yet apparently incorporated a bedroom, kitchen and living area, his brain was waking up and his senses were returning. He could hear the sink tap dripping rhythmically. The musty smell of damp invaded his nostrils. Behind him, the door opened and then closed behind the friend he distantly recalled being introduced to as Carla Blake, who'd been minding Josh while Georgie pitched up on his doorstep and exploded a world already off kilter.

Yet his focus was all on the cot in the corner and the child lying within it.

As he slowly walked towards it, his pulse pounded and his mouth went dry. He gripped the top rail, his knuckles white, and looked down. At the sight of the baby, lying on his back with his chubby arms out and his tiny hands curled into loose fists, his breath caught and his chest clenched.

'Do you want to pick him up?' he heard Georgie say quietly in the gloomy darkness that was illuminated by one bare lightbulb.

No. Yes. More than anything. 'I don't want to disturb him,' he said gruffly, mesmerised by the gentle rise and fall of the blanket that covered the little body.

'You won't. He takes a while to settle but once he's out, he's out. Just make sure you support his head.'

He reached down and lifted the bundle of warm baby and bedclothes to him, his throat tight. Josh snuffled and then settled against his chest, and he felt the warmth of his son's body seep into every inch of him, filling him with an emotion he didn't recognise and couldn't begin to describe.

He was so tiny, so vulnerable. And only six months old. The same age as Finn had been when he'd been adopted. Who could give up something so precious?

And why would someone want to? Had he been too difficult? Too demanding? Had his biological mother needed help in the same way it seemed Georgie did, if her descent from glorious, kick-ass girl-about-town to nervous, ghostly wreck was anything to go by? Had his own mother not had it?

Yet more unanswerable questions.

But this wasn't about him right now. This was about the baby he was holding. Already, there was nothing he wouldn't do for this child, he thought with a burning conviction he could hardly comprehend. Nothing. Never mind that he had no experience of babies. Never mind that he hadn't ever wanted responsibility of this kind before. He had it now and, whatever the circumstances, he would never abandon Josh. He would never give up responsibility for him. His son would never have cause to wonder who he was or where he came from. His son, his flesh and blood and, as far as he knew the only relative he had left in the world, would have everything that was in his power to give. And be. Because Finn may or may not have been good enough for either his biological or adoptive parents, but he'd do his damnedest to be the best for his son.

Here was his chance to right past wrongs. To try and move on from the still raw sense of betrayal and rejection he felt. To plan and to build and to focus on something greater. He was no longer alone. He now had a purpose beyond work and an escape from the chaos. And as he bent to settle the baby back in the cot, missing his sweet smell and soft weight already, he realised that, for the first time in months, the way forward was crystal clear. On this, at least, he knew exactly what to do.

Pushing aside messy, incomprehensible emotion and replacing it with easier to understand practicality, Finn straightened and turned to face Georgie, who was leaning against the one kitchen unit that the bedsit contained, looking oddly flushed and on edge.

'Here's what's going to happen,' he said, watching as her chin came up and her eyes narrowed slightly at his tone.

'Oh, yes?'

'Josh is coming home with me.'

She blinked. 'What?'

'This place isn't fit for habitation.'

'I know.'

'It's a health hazard.'

'I know.'

'He's not staying here.'

'Well, he's going nowhere without me,' she countered, and for the briefest of moments Finn toyed with the idea of telling her that he could easily take Josh without her. That he had the power and resources to remove her from the picture altogether, especially in view of her straitened circumstances, and could do so with a click of his fingers.

But he knew what it was like to grow up without a maternal figure and the gaping hole that had left in his life. The man he'd considered his father had

done his best, but Finn had no doubt that much of
the trouble he'd got into as a teenager had been an
outlet for the delayed rage and injustice he'd felt at
his mother's loss.

And then there was the situation he was currently
in. He'd been denied the truth about his parentage
and as a result now seethed with resentment and frustration. He wouldn't wish the torment he'd experienced as a boy and was now experiencing all over
again on anyone, least of all his own child. Therefore, while Georgie was an added complication, she
was a necessary one.

'Alright,' he said. 'You come too. Get what you
need for tonight and I'll have the rest of your things
moved to my place in the morning.'

'For how long?'

'Until we figure out what happens next.'

'We?'

At the question in her voice, Finn inwardly tensed.
He'd never been part of a 'we' before. He'd never
had to be, never wanted to be, had no clue how to
be. But so much of his life had become uncharted
territory recently, what was one patch more? 'We,'
he confirmed with a brief nod before stalking over
to the cupboard and reaching up to pull down a bag
that had been stashed on top of it. 'Start packing.
You have five minutes.'

Since her bedsit was minuscule and the possessions
she had with her meagre, Georgie took only four

minutes, and one of those she spent arguing with herself.

The old her would have protested loudly at being ordered around in such an autocratic fashion. She'd have demanded to know who Finn thought he was and what century he was living in before telling him where to go and shoving him out the door. But, while part of her wished she had the energy to conjure up that version of herself, the other part of her, the current Georgie, the one that was exhausted and desperate, whose judgement was skewed and who couldn't trust herself, was too grateful to put up any kind of a fight. To have someone else make the decisions and take responsibility was such a relief. Finn's authority and decisiveness imbued her with the confidence that if something should happen to her, her son would be safe. After months of not being able to make choices, she'd finally made the right one. She and Josh badly needed rescuing, and Finn being the one to do it was absolutely fine with her.

Besides, he clearly wasn't planning to leave without them and the last thing she wanted was a standoff leading to more time spent in this place. The flat was small enough without Finn in it. With him in it, it felt even more claustrophobic. There was just so much of him too close. His size and proximity and sheer presence made her aware of him and the narrow bed in a way she hadn't expected and definitely wasn't comfortable with. When he'd lifted Josh out of the cot, and held his son's tiny body against his big, broad chest, her stomach had clenched and her entire body had flushed.

Now, as she moved around the space, around *him*, gathering the things she and Josh needed, she could feel his cool, assessing eyes on her, and his scrutiny caused her skin to prickle and a strange heat to seep through her. Not that it mattered how Finn made her feel. Even if he *had* been interested in her in the way he once had been, which clearly and thankfully he was not, she was far too fragile for that sort of thing these days, so it was just as well her libido had gone AWOL. And, besides, she had other, far more important things to focus on now.

Zipping up the bag, Georgie handed it to Finn and went to pick up their son. From above there came an ominous thud followed by a loud crash that made her jump. And as she locked the front door of the bedsit and followed Finn down the dimly lit stairs she thought that whatever his reaction when he eventually learned the truth, however precarious her position in all this, the future had to better than the past.

What a night.

A couple of hours ago all Finn had had to worry about was the frustrating lack of results the investigation into his adoption had generated. Now he had a son being tucked up in one of his spare rooms by an unexpected house guest, and he was pacing up and down in front of the wall-to-wall windows of his sitting room wondering what more the universe could possibly hurl at him. Battered didn't come close to describing how he felt about everything that had happened this evening. He'd been on the receiving end of one punch to the gut after another, and, quite frankly, how he was still standing he had no idea.

And that wasn't all he couldn't fathom. There was also the conundrum that was Georgie. What had happened to her? he wondered as he strode to the drinks cabinet and poured himself a large Scotch. When they'd originally met she'd been vivacious and sassy and intoxicating, out celebrating her twenty-fifth birthday with friends. She'd told him she worked as a lawyer specialising in defamation, that she'd just been promoted and had her eye on a partnership. She'd been living in Kensal Rise, and he specifically recalled her telling him, out there on the street in between hot, drugging kisses, that if they wanted privacy the flat she shared with three others was not the place to go.

Clearly she'd fallen on hard times, but how, and why? She'd had a baby, yes, but that wouldn't have felled the Georgie he'd met fifteen months ago. That girl would have taken a baby in her stride and carried on conquering the world.

And, on the subject of timings, why was he only finding out about his son now? Why had she taken so long to contact him? Why the secrecy? He couldn't stand secrets. Ignorance put a man at a disadvantage. It robbed him of control and rendered him powerless and weak, and he should know because he was living it.

Well, he'd had enough of being kept in the dark, he thought, knocking back half his drink and resuming his pacing. The issues surrounding his adoption aside, he had a multitude of questions to ask Georgie about Josh, and the minute she reappeared he was getting an answer to every single one of them, whether she liked it or not.

CHAPTER THREE

OBLIVIOUS TO THE drama going on around him and having remained asleep throughout, Josh handled the move to Finn's place with ease. Georgie, on the other hand, was having slightly more trouble adjusting.

She'd been too relieved to see the back of the bedsit to give much thought to where Finn might be taking them, but even if she had, the seven-star hotel where they'd spent that wild night together would not have crossed her mind. Yet here they were, in the penthouse, no less, which boasted a stunning sitting room, a state-of-the-art kitchen, a library and a terrace. The upper level comprised of three en-suite bedrooms—two of which were interconnecting—and a separate wing that had been presumably designed for staff. The chandeliers were crystal and the linen on her bed felt as though it had a thousand thread count. The walls throughout were painted a soft white, and neutral rugs covered glossy dark oak floorboards.

The whole apartment smelled divine and the sense of peace and tranquillity was like a balm to her soul.

She couldn't imagine a greater contrast to either the bedsit or the mother-and-baby unit of the psychiatric ward where she'd spent close on five months, and once again a wave of gratitude and relief washed over her, along with a hefty dose of curiosity. Who exactly was he, her knight in shining armour who owned a nightclub, drove a Lamborghini and lived in a seven-star penthouse?

Leaving the door to Josh's room ajar in case he needed her, Georgie went down the stairs, crossed the hall and stopped in the doorway to the sitting room. Finn was pacing up and down in front of the window, a near-empty glass in his hand and a deep frown creasing his forehead. When he saw her, he came to an abrupt halt. His jaw was set, his eyes were dark and intense, and something in his expression, in the way he was looking at her, sent a shiver down her spine.

'Is everything all right?' he said.

'Everything is very all right,' she replied, ignoring the shiver and mustering up her second smile of the day, which had to be a record. 'I just wanted to say thank you for everything you've done.'

'You're welcome.'

'You have no idea how grateful I am for your support.'

'Josh is my son.'

And what was she? An inconvenience? Undoubtedly. Finn didn't even want her here, she knew, remembering how he'd grudgingly told her she could come too when she'd swiftly disabused him of the idea that he'd be taking Josh without her.

'I didn't realise you actually lived here,' she said, dragging her gaze from his to sweep it around the room upon whose threshold she was hovering. 'When we met you said you were renovating. I assumed your stay was temporary.'

'I was, and in that room it was temporary.'

'But why live in a hotel?'

'Why not? I own it.'

Her gaze snapped back to his and her jaw dropped. 'You *own* it?'

'Yes.'

'As well as the club where we met?'

He gave a brief nod. 'Among other things.'

'Who *are* you?' she said, thinking that in hindsight it was a question she should have asked him last October. She still didn't even know his last name. She'd had to leave that space on Josh's birth certificate blank.

He muttered something that sounded remarkably like 'Good question', which made no sense all, but then added something that did. 'Finn Calvert,' he said. 'Look me up some time. Right now, though, we need to talk. Or rather, you do.'

As his gaze drilled into her Georgie went still, her pulse beginning to thud alarmingly fast. 'Oh, well, I really just came to say thank you and goodnight. It's been quite a day.'

'You're telling me.'

'I'm exhausted.'

'Too bad.'

'Any chance we could talk tomorrow?'

'No.'

She stuck her hands into the back pockets of her jeans and shifted her weight from one foot to the other. 'Because, ah, you know, I think I hear Josh crying.'

'No, you don't,' he said, the brusqueness of his tone reflecting the flint in his expression. 'Carry on prevaricating, Georgie, and I'll have a team of investigators looking into you so fast it'll make your head spin.'

Her eyes widened. 'Are you serious?'

'One phone call. That's all it will take. I have them on speed dial.'

Why would Finn have investigators on speed dial? was her instant thought in response to that, but it was a question for later. Because clearly the moment she'd been dreading had come. Would he really get her checked out? Or was he bluffing? Either way, it didn't really matter. She couldn't take the risk that he would do precisely as he threatened. She needed to control the narrative. She needed to provide context and detail to the cold, clinical facts. It was important that Finn understood exactly what she'd been through and sympathised. She needed him on her side. It wasn't going to be easy. In fact, it was probably going to be hell, but it had to be done.

'All right,' she said with a nod as her stomach began to churn.

'Sit down.'

On legs that felt as weak as water Georgie walked over to the sofa Finn indicated and perched on the edge of it, because to sink back into the soft cushions would result in an inadvisable degree of relaxation. She waited until he'd folded himself into one of the armchairs on the other side of the coffee table, then took a deep breath. She opened her mouth, then closed it and gave a helpless shrug. 'I'm not quite sure where to start.'

'How about by telling me why I am *only now* finding out I have a six-month-old son?'

She inwardly flinched at his tone, but it was as good a place to start as any, so she pulled herself together and mentally spooled back to the beginning. 'As I told you earlier this evening,' she said, deciding to start with the marginally easier bit, 'you're a hard man to track down.'

'You've had fifteen months.'

'Not quite.'

His brows snapped together. 'What do you mean?'

'I didn't know I was pregnant until I went into hospital with severe stomach cramps back in July and had Josh four hours later.'

The silence that suddenly fell vibrated between them, laden with astonishment and disbelief. The tick of the clock on the mantelpiece, marking the passing of the seconds that felt like minutes, was deafening.

'You didn't know you were pregnant?' he echoed eventually, the intensity of his gaze pinning her to the spot and making her squirm.

'No.'

'How is that even possible?'

'That's a question I've asked myself many times.'

'And?'

'I apparently had what's called a cryptic pregnancy,' she said, rubbing her damp palms down her denim-clad thighs. 'I carried on taking the pill, so I didn't miss a period. I didn't have morning sickness or any other signs. Because I was so busy at work I was exhausted anyway. Maybe I ate a bit more and gained a couple of pounds, but I put it down to stress-related comfort eating and cut back.' She paused to give him time to at least partly absorb what she'd said, then added, 'I realise how this must sound.'

'You can't have any idea how this sounds,' he said darkly. 'Implausible doesn't come anywhere near it.'

She couldn't blame him for his scepticism. If she'd been in his shoes she'd have dismissed the idea as ridiculous too. 'It's rare but it happens. To one in about two thousand five hundred women. I had an anterior placenta. If I ever felt any movements, I put them down to tummy rumbles. I really had no idea. When my waters broke and I started having contractions right in the middle of A&E, no one was more surprised than me.'

And wasn't that an understatement? Stunned and terrified was a more accurate description of the feelings that had stormed through her. She'd never felt physical pain like it. She'd thought she was dying. And then, when realisation had dawned, the awful, horrible confusion. How could she be pregnant? How could she not have known that she was? She wasn't stupid. She wasn't uneducated. Yet in those bewildering, petrifying moments she'd felt both.

'And subsequently?' he said bluntly, yanking her out of the chaos and confusion of the delivery room and back to the present. 'Josh is six months old.'

'The whole thing came as a massive shock to me,' she said, remembering with a chill how quickly and devastatingly her smooth, well-ordered life had been blown apart. 'I was totally unprepared. I hadn't been to any antenatal classes. I'd read no books and looked nothing up. I had no baby things and absolutely no idea what I was doing. I was thrown in at the deep end and expected to swim. It's been a busy time and insanely tough.'

His dark gaze held hers, not allowing her to look away, not letting her off the hook for one second. 'Still, Georgie. Six months.'

'I know.'

'Well?'

This was it. Her moment of reckoning. 'Could I possibly have a drink? I'm not prevaricating,' she added in response to the sharp arch of his eyebrow. 'Truly. I could just do with a bit of fortification.'

'That bad?'

Worse. 'Maybe.'

'What would you like?'

'Whatever you're having.'

'Scotch.'

'That'll do. Neat. No ice.'

With a brief nod, Finn got to his feet and strode over to the bar to fix her drink and refill his while Georgie tried to marshal her thoughts, her mouth dry and her heart pounding. How much should she tell him? What could she leave out? Was there anything she could do to make this easier? Unlikely.

'Thank you,' she said, accepting the glass he held out and taking a long, slow sip of the whisky. 'Delicious. Peaty.'

The look he gave her was forbidding, his patience clearly stretched. 'Georgie.'

Right. OK. She lowered her glass and braced herself for the guilt and shame and anguish that still crucified her even though she knew that none of it had been her fault. 'So, as I said,' she said, her voice shaking a little despite her efforts to control it, 'Josh's arrival was unexpected. It was also extremely traumatic. Not from a medical point of view—in those terms it was very easy apparently—but from a mental one. I'd left home that morning expecting to be given some strong prescription painkillers. I'd envisaged being back in time to finish the report I'd been working on. Instead, ten hours after being admitted, I went home with a tiny newborn baby.'

She looked at him, willing him to at least try to understand, however big an ask that was. 'The shock was cataclysmic. I can't begin to describe the weight of responsibility. Or the terror. I was all on my own and I had no clue what to do. I didn't know how to feed him or soothe him or anything. For forty-eight hours neither of us slept, which meant that nor did my flatmates, who were quick to point out I was now in contravention of the tenancy agreement and threatened to call the landlord.'

She glanced down at the glass she was turning in her hands, the amber liquid swirling continuously. 'I phoned my parents but they didn't answer, which I more or less expected, since we hadn't spoken for a while, so I rang Carla, the friend of mine you met earlier. She came over and scooped us up and took us back to her house. And that was great for a couple of days. I scoured the internet and read books and did a crash course in babies. And I got a bit better at changing Josh's nappies and feeding him and generally looking after him. But as the shock wore off, reality kicked in.' She looked up at Finn, who was sitting impossibly still, his eyes dark and his expression unreadable, although she guessed he wasn't missing a thing. 'Did I ever mention my five-year plan?' she asked with a slight tilt of her head.

'You mentioned having one.'

'Well, that went out the window. And so did all the structure and routine I'd created for myself and have always depended on. My life fell completely apart, and for the first time in years I had no idea where I was heading.' She shook her head, the memories swirling. 'It was all so overwhelming. I went into a sort of spin and it happened really quickly and really intensely. I wasn't sleeping much anyway, but suddenly I wasn't sleeping at all. My appetite all but disappeared. And then I started doing things that were really out of character. Like talking really fast one minute then not uttering a word for hours. I developed panic attacks and became convinced that Carla's neighbour was following me. I even called the police one night,' she said, biting her lip and remembering how scary it had been to realise on some level that what she was doing wasn't normal, wasn't right, but not knowing why she was doing it and not being able to do anything about it. 'Anyway, eventually I was admitted to the psychiatric ward of my local hospital, where I was diagnosed with postpartum psychosis.'

'Which is what?'

'Like postnatal depression but worse.' Far, *far* worse. 'I stayed there for a week and then a bed came up in a mother-and-baby unit a hundred miles away. Josh and I left there ten days ago,' she said, glossing over five intervening months, since Finn did not need to know how bad it had got before the medication had kicked in and the therapy had started to take effect. In any case she doubted she could even begin to explain how terrifying the delusions and the hallucinations and the disorientation had been, or how distressing she'd found it knowing that she wasn't well. The feelings she'd had for Josh, or, rather, the lack of them, were far too upsetting to put into words, and

Finn would never understand her gut-churning dread that the long, dark tunnel she'd been in had no end. He'd never fully understand any of it. No one could.

'And that's why it's taken so long for me to contact you,' she said, determinedly not letting those agonising memories descend but instead focusing on the man who was now looking at her a little as though he'd been slapped round the head with a wet fish. 'I wasn't in a position to do so. As soon as I was, I did. And that's it. Now you know everything.'

Everything? *Everything*?

He knew *nothing*.

Watching dazedly as Georgie finished her drink, set the glass down on the coffee table and sat back against the cushions, Finn could barely recall his own *name*. He was reeling too hard, too stunned and shattered to be able to make head or tail of anything. Whatever explanation he could possibly have envisaged, none would have come anywhere near the one she'd just given him.

That she was telling the truth was without doubt. He might have had suspicions initially—who wouldn't?—but not for long. No one would make up such a story, and no one could fake the emotion that had emanated from her, despite her attempts to contain it. When she'd been talking about what she'd been through, her voice had cracked and her eyes had become twin pools of pain. Her hands had trembled and her anguish had been palpable, and her obvious distress had cut right through him.

On one level he could identify with some of what had initially happened to her. He knew what it was like to have your life turned upside down and your plans destroyed. He'd experienced the sort of catastrophic shock that imploded your world, and the subsequent feeling of being utterly at sea. In that respect their recent histories were not unalike.

As for the rest, however, he couldn't *begin* to imagine what she'd been through. He thought he'd been having a rough time, but compared with her past six months, his had been a breeze. Giving birth like that must have been terrifying. Finding herself wholly and solely responsible for a tiny, helpless human being that came with no instruction manual must have been petrifying.

And then afterwards… God, he didn't even know what post-partum psychosis was. But it sounded horrendous, like hell on earth. Georgie hadn't gone into detail about her stay in hospital but what she *had* revealed had been harrowing to listen to, let alone to actually live through, so how had she got through it? *Had* she got through it? Well, clearly she'd recovered at least to *some* extent because she and Josh were here, not that it was any thanks to him.

He should have been there, he thought, a white-hot streak of regret and guilt suddenly burning through the defences he hadn't had time to shore up. He should have known. Never mind that he couldn't have. Never mind that her recent experience was no one's fault, not even his. And never mind that even if he *had* been around he probably wouldn't have known her well enough to recognise the out-of-character behaviour or any of the other signs that indicated she was ill.

What mattered was that he hadn't been there for his father, and he hadn't been there for Georgie and Josh either. History had apparently repeated itself and that ended right now because, while he hadn't been able to help his father or the Georgie of then, he *could* help her now. In whatever way she needed, whenever she needed it. He wouldn't let her, *them*, down.

'How are you doing now?' he asked gruffly, aware suddenly that she was looking at him with the expectation of some sort of response.

'Better. Much better.'

'And Josh?'

She released a long, slow breath and the troubled expression that flitted across her face made his chest tighten with renewed regret that things hadn't been different for her.

'I'd like to be able to say that I've totally bonded with him and everything's great,' she said carefully. 'But the truth is that, while I *am* getting there, it's a work in progress. For a long time I couldn't look after him properly. I couldn't even look after myself. He was cared for by hospital staff so we didn't get a chance to create that connection that everyone talks about and I missed many milestones.' She shifted on the sofa and frowned for a moment as if something had suddenly occurred to her. 'But maybe subconsciously I knew that there'd be a time when I was OK because I took photos and kept a diary. I did everything that was recommended. And I think it's working. Now I find him fascinating. I can't imagine not having him around, and when I think… Well… I'd rather not think about any of it actually.'

As she tailed off Finn could see the undeserved guilt and shame in her eyes, which deepened his regret, but he could also recall the fire in her expression when she'd stood there in her flat and told him that Josh was going nowhere without her. Perhaps the bond between them was stronger than she was able to recognise right now.

And, seeing as how he was now thinking about where she and their son had been living… 'How on earth did you end up in the bedsit?' he asked, seeking some sort of refuge from the emotions battering him by switching to practicalities.

Georgie blinked at the sudden change in subject and visibly shuddered. 'It was all I could afford.'

'What happened to your job?'

'A couple of weeks after I was admitted to hospital I got an email from my company saying that as a result of restructuring my position no longer existed.'

He frowned. 'A coincidence?'

'I doubt it. But I was in no state to object. The pay-off was pathetic.'

Bastards. 'What about your parents?'

She gave a wry smile. 'Even if we were on speaking terms, a hippie commune is the very last place I would choose to raise a child. Believe me, I have first-hand experience and it wasn't all that great.'

'Friends?'

'It's all been too much for many of them and I was too far away. And I couldn't ask any more of Carla. She'd already done so much…' She paused for a second, swallowing hard as a quick frown creased her brow, seemingly lost in thought, but a second later she'd rallied. 'Besides, she has her own life to lead. Her job is insane.'

'Remind me to thank her some time,' he muttered, not wanting to even think about how alone Georgie had been, how desperate she must have felt.

'She's going to be intrigued by this latest turn of events. If she wasn't going away for work tomorrow I have no doubt she'd be banging on the door first thing.'

'She's welcome any time.'

For a moment she didn't say anything, just looked at him, her eyes shimmering with gratitude that he did not deserve when his help had come so late. 'You have no idea how glad I am to have found you.'

His pulse thudded heavily and something shifted in his chest. 'Likewise.'

'You may not think that when Josh is screaming the place down.'

'The walls are soundproofed.'

'That's a relief.' She gave him a faint smile. 'So. Is there anything else you'd like to know?'

Probably. No doubt there were questions he hadn't even thought of. But in all honesty he couldn't take any more tonight. He was utterly drained. God only knew how she had the strength to smile after everything she'd just told him. But then, compared with what had come before, he supposed relaying an account of it would have been a walk in the park. Her courage was staggering. Her resilience was a thing of awe. He'd thought that he was pretty tough, but he had nothing on her. He had nothing at all. 'We'll talk more in the morning.'

CHAPTER FOUR

WHILE GEORGIE GOT ready for bed she reflected that, as she'd suspected, it hadn't been easy telling Finn her story. In fact, reliving events even on the most superficial level had been horrible and exhausting. But it had also been cathartic. The weight and severity of what she'd been through had been overwhelming and now that she'd shared some of it she felt slightly lighter, as if a socking great rock was beginning to lift from her shoulders.

It had helped that Finn was such a good listener. He'd offered no opinion and no judgement. He'd just sat there letting her talk. Of course, it was entirely probable that there'd simply been too much to take in for him to be able to respond with anything more than the most basic of questions, but nevertheless she was grateful for his restraint. And his involvement. It was such a relief to know that she was no longer in this alone, but who exactly was she in it with?

Remembering his suggestion to look him up, Georgie fished her phone out of her bag, then climbed under the gorgeously soft covers of the enormous bed. She tapped his name—complete with surname—into a search engine and spent the next fifteen minutes clicking on links and reading articles.

But, instead of cementing the feeling of safety and security that had been burgeoning inside her, what she discovered blew it wide apart. Because, while she'd already guessed that Finn was successful—what with owning a hotel and a club, driving a top-of-the-range car and living in a penthouse—never in her wildest nightmares would she have imagined that he was one of the richest men in the world.

Yet he was.

His company owned hotels and bars and clubs and restaurants and he was worth billions. He'd worked his way up from virtually nothing to become a top player in his industry. His power was immense and his influence was wide-reaching, and it was suddenly terrifying because now she couldn't help thinking that what if, once he'd had time to absorb the truth about where she'd been and what she'd been doing for the last six months and reflect on it, he considered her unfit to be a mother to his son? What if he tried to take Josh away from her in earnest? She wouldn't stand a chance. If it came to a custody battle, a judge would take one look at her with her recent mental health record and another at Finn with his billions and that would be that. Case closed. She was sure of it.

She'd gone into so much detail, she thought, a wave of nausea rolling up from her stomach to her throat. About her behaviour. About her conflicted feelings towards Josh. She hadn't told him the worst of what had happened, but it had been enough. More than enough.

Her vision blurred and a cold sweat broke out all over her skin at the thought of how much she'd revealed, how vulnerable she'd made herself. What had seemed such a relief a mere half an hour ago now felt like the biggest mistake of her life. What did he think about it all? What could he be plotting? How could she possibly sleep, not knowing what he intended to do next? Morning was too far away. She needed clarification now.

Throwing back the covers, Georgie leapt out of bed and crossed the hall. When she reached his room she didn't think to knock; all she could focus on was protecting Josh and herself and fighting her corner. She opened the door and strode in. Finn was standing next to the bed, wearing a look of surprise on his face and nothing but a towel wrapped around his hips.

'I have one more thing to say,' she said hoarsely, barely able to hear her own voice above the thundering of her heart, 'and it can't wait until morning.'

'What is it?'

'I am not perfect. I am still in recovery. But I can do this. And I am capable. I am not a risk to either myself or Josh and I never will be. I will not let you take my son away from me. I will *never* let you take him away from me.' She stopped, breathing hard, the force of the emotion swirling through her nearly knocking her off her feet.

'What are you talking about?' he said with a frown. 'I have no intention of taking him away from you.'

'You did earlier,' she fired back. 'In the bedsit.'

'Yet here you are.'

His dark, steady gaze was locked on hers and something in it, together with the very valid point he'd just made, calmed some of the wildness whipping about inside her. 'How can I believe you?'

'You have my word.'

'I don't know you well enough yet to know if that means anything.'

'Then you'll just have to trust me.'

'How can I?'

'My mother died when I was ten,' he said, a shadow flitting across his face. 'I know what it's like to grow up without one. It is not something I'd ever wish to inflict on my own son. Josh will always know both his parents.'

His words sank in and she swallowed hard. 'Do you really mean that?'

'I do,' he said with a brief nod.

'OK, then,' she said, letting out a breath as the tension and steam inside her eased. 'Good. Thank you.'

'Was there anything else?'

'Ah, no. Sorry to barge in like that. I didn't realise you were…' What? What had he been doing? Her gaze, which had been fixed firmly to his, broke away to travel over the rest of him. His hair was damp. The exposed skin of his broad, muscled chest gleamed in the soft golden light of the room. He'd clearly just come out of the shower, and, now that she wasn't all fired up with needing to say her piece, it hit her with the force of a freight train that she was standing in his bedroom and he was practically naked.

'…In the middle of something,' she finished lamely, feeling her cheeks burn as she dragged her eyes back up.

'Obviously not.'

'Sorry.'

'Next time, knock.'

There wouldn't be a next time. 'Right. Yes.' She cleared her throat. 'Of course. Sorry. Again.'

His dark blue gaze glittered. 'Goodnight, Georgie.'

'Goodnight.'

When Georgie woke up the following morning, it was with great reluctance. Not only was she so warm and cosy she didn't want to leave the cocoon she'd fashioned out of the duvet, but she was also still utterly wiped out.

It had taken her a long while to fall asleep. She hadn't been able to stop thinking about everything that had happened the evening before, starting with the moment Finn's bouncer had told her to stop and wait. She could scarcely believe any of what had subsequently unfolded was real, yet here she was, safe and warm and no longer wretched and desperate and on her own.

And then there were the dreams she'd had once she *had* managed to drift off, dreams that seemed to involve her and Finn and what might have happened if, instead of fleeing his room, she'd walked up to him and rid him of his towel. Details of what followed were hazy and the whole idea of it was absurd, of course, but nevertheless, why she should be going there, even subconsciously, was a bit baffling.

As was the fact that light was streaming in through the blinds, which, seeing as how it was January, meant that it must be late.

Too late.

And too quiet.

And then mid-yawn, mid-stretch, it suddenly struck Georgie that she'd woken of her own accord and she froze, panic coursing through her. Why hadn't Josh woken her as usual?

Something was wrong.

Icy cold and shaking, she threw back the duvet and leapt out of bed. She raced to his cot in the room next door, only to find it empty.

Where was he? Who had taken him? What had Finn done?

Terror gripped every inch of her. Her knees gave way and she had to cling to the rail of the cot to stop crumpling to the floor. Her heart was thundering and she felt as if she'd been cleaved in two. She couldn't have lost her son, having only just found him. Fate couldn't be that cruel. But where had he gone? What was she going to do?

And then a burst of sound pierced the fog of alarm and desperation, rooting her to the spot and pricking her ears.

A gurgle. A stream of giggles. A low masculine voice.

Slowly coming out of her daze, Georgie felt reason return and the terror subside. Josh was OK. Everything was all right.

Still trembling, her pulse still racing, she followed the sounds to the glossy kitchen, where she found Josh sitting in a brand-new pristine high chair, with Finn beside him, feeding him. Upon the black granite worktop that looked as if it had never met so much as a chopping board sat plastic bottles and tubs of milk powder, bibs and muslins, tiny plates and cutlery, all the paraphernalia an infant required and lots more besides.

Stunned into immobility, she watched Finn expertly spoon food into Josh's waiting mouth, with hardly any of it splattering onto the tray or the floor, and to her shame she felt a surge of resentment. Where had all this stuff come from? How did Finn know in less than twenty-four hours what it had taken her months to figure out? She'd found feeding her son unbelievably fraught. She'd been riddled with anxiety and uncertainty, convinced she was somehow going to poison him by getting the proportions wrong. She still was on occasion. Yet Finn made it look so easy. Unfair didn't *begin* to describe the situation.

'Good morning,' he said, shooting her a dark glance which he then raked over her, his jaw tightening minutely. 'Did you sleep well?'

Ish… 'Yes,' she replied, ignoring his obvious, if unfathomable, objection to her pyjamas. 'Did you?'

He muttered something non-committal and turned his attention back to Josh. 'Help yourself to some breakfast.'

She looked in the direction in which he'd nodded, and at the sight of the array of pastries and fruit enticingly arranged on a great silver platter her mouth watered and her stomach rumbled. God, it had been a long time since she'd come across anything so appetising. She filled a plate and then took a seat opposite him.

'How long has Josh been up?' she asked, pouring herself some coffee and taking a fortifying sip.

'A couple of hours.'

She frowned. 'I didn't hear him.'

'You were dead to the world.'

'But you weren't.'

'No. I was doing some research.'

No need to ask into what.

'And some thinking.'

'Oh?' she said, picking up a *pain au chocolat*. 'About what?'

'What happens next.'

'Which is?' She took a bite and nearly groaned with pleasure.

'Firstly,' he said, his gaze dipping to her mouth for a second and darkening, 'I've hired a nanny.'

Georgie nearly choked on a flake of pastry. A nanny? Why would he do that? Didn't he trust her? Didn't he think she could cope? Just because she'd had a lie-in this morning didn't mean she couldn't. And what else had he unilaterally arranged? Lawyers? Psychiatrists? What? Her heart was beating too fast. Her breathing was too shallow. She had to calm down.

'I said I could do this,' she told him, her mouth dry and the *pain au chocolat* turning to lead in her stomach.

'I don't doubt it,' he replied, all steady calm and cool self-assurance.

'Are you sure about that?'

'Yes. However, you've been ill. You need rest.'

'I need to be with Josh. We need to strengthen our bond.'

'I suspect your bond is stronger than you realise.'

At that, hot anger flared into life inside her. How dared he be so patronising? What did he know about anything? One night of research and he was an expert? She didn't think so.

'Another stranger in his life will be confusing,' she said, ignoring the tiny stab of guilt she felt when he visibly flinched. 'I don't want a nanny looking after my son. I don't need that kind of help.'

'Well, perhaps I do,' he countered with a bluntness that whipped the wind from her sails.

This wasn't just about her any more, she realised with a shock. She had to consider the situation from his point of view too. His life had irrevocably changed overnight. This was new territory for him. She had to give him a break. And maybe, on occasion, she *did* need the kind of help a nanny would provide.

'When does she start?'

'The day after tomorrow.'

'Full-time?'

'Days only.'

'OK, fine,' she said, a bit grudgingly nevertheless. 'But you should have discussed it with me first.'

He gave her a long look and then gave a brief nod. 'My mistake.'

'From what I read last night, you don't make mistakes.'

'This isn't business.'

'No.' Although quite what it was she had no idea. 'And secondly?'

'Secondly, I'm taking some time off work.'

Oh? At the thought of him being around to witness her struggles and her ineptitude, her skin prickled. But, seeing as how she'd requested his support and he'd supplied it, she could hardly protest. 'I read you were a workaholic.'

'That was before I became a father,' he said, glancing at Josh, who was banging a spoon on the tray of his high chair, his expression softening a fraction. 'I intend to get to know my son. Everything he is and everything he does. Nothing is more important.'

He meant it too, Georgie thought, her resentment morphing into wistfulness as she watched Finn watching his son with an intensity and interest she'd never had from either of her parents. It was silly and slightly shameful to be jealous of a six-month-old, but there it was.

'You'll need to show me what to do,' he added, sliding his gaze back to her, the lingering warmth in his eyes easing some of the numbness that filled so much of her.

'*You're* asking *me* for advice?' she said with a quick glance at the extensive baby kit he'd somehow masterfully amassed.

'You have a head start on me.'

'Not much of one.'

'Yes, well, I know nothing. Before last night I'd never been this close to a baby, let alone had to take care of one.'

Slightly taken aback by his frank admission, because in her experience rare was the man who confessed he needed help, although she supposed that, unlike many men of her acquaintance, Finn had nothing to prove, she asked, 'So where did all this come from?'

'My COO's off on maternity leave. I called her and she sent me a list of essentials. And that's it.'

It was strangely reassuring to know that she wasn't the only one at sea. 'Well, I'll *try.*'

'OK, then,' he said, flashing her a sudden smile that lit up his whole face and momentarily dazzled her. 'Let's do this.'

An hour later, Finn found himself in Josh's room, grappling with the concept of a wriggly, giggly child, a nappy that needed changing and not enough hands.

How could such a simple thing be so difficult? Georgie had told him what to do before heading off for a bath and it hadn't seemed that complicated, yet he'd been at it for ten minutes now with no success. His company tax returns were easier to get a handle on than this.

Nevertheless, there was absolutely nothing he'd rather be doing. One of the many reasons it was taking so long and proving so tricky was because he kept being distracted by his son. He'd only just managed to lay him flat when he'd found himself transfixed by the curve of his right eyebrow for a good thirty seconds, by which point Josh had kicked several crucial pieces of equipment to the floor and they'd had to start all over again.

At least Georgie had left him to it and wasn't around to witness his rare incompetence and his even rarer sentimental fascination with another human being. With any luck she had no idea either of how her brief but disturbing foray into his bedroom last night had affected him. In she'd barged, all stunningly fired up one moment and then staring at him as if she wanted to gobble him up the next. He'd caught a flash of hunger in her eyes and heard the breathlessness of her voice, and a reciprocal burst of hot, dizzying desire had shot through him. After she'd left he'd had to take another shower, a cold one, and he had the feeling that he'd be taking many more if his response to how she'd looked walking into the kitchen this morning, all warm and flushed and tousled, was anything to go by.

Finally achieving the impossible and sticking the nappy tabs in the right places and then somehow managing to guide two wriggling legs back into a pair of tiny trousers, Finn lifted Josh off the table. As he did so their eyes met and held, and as they stared at each other, stock still and fascinated, he felt something deep inside him twist. The physical similarities he and his son shared were startling. He hadn't resembled either Alice or Jim at all. And suddenly he wondered, did he look like either or both of his biological parents? Did he have his father's nose? His mother's eyes? A grandparent's mouth? Would he recognise them if he ever had the chance to meet them? Would they have the same connection he felt with Josh?

Would he *ever* find the answers he sought?

'How did you get on?' said Georgie, coming into what was now the nursery and snapping him out of his impossibly frustrating thoughts.

'It's harder than it looks.'

'You'll get the hang of it. If I can, anyone can.'

Hmm. 'Did you want something?'

'The rest of my things have just arrived. I was wondering if you'd like to see the photos of Josh that I took while we were in hospital.'

'I would.'

She took a couple of steps towards him until she was closer—too close—and shifted her glance from him to Josh. 'He looks so like you,' she said, her voice filled with warmth and softness.

He took a step back, his pulse skipping a beat. 'Yes.'

'Maybe we could compare pictures. Of both of you as newborns.'

Impossible. There weren't any of him at that age. When going through his father's attic he'd found a few photos of himself at six months old, and endless photos of himself older than Josh was now, but none younger, which he'd wondered about until he'd found the certificate of his adoption and it all made sense. 'Another time.'

'All right.'

'I'd like you to talk me through Josh's routine,' he said, carrying his son out of the nursery, which was far too small and claustrophobic with Georgie in it too, down the stairs and into the sitting room.

'To be honest, he doesn't really have one.'

'Do you want him to?'

'More than anything. What do you think?'

'I'm as big a fan of structure as you are.'

'Be still my beating heart.'

And, as his gave a great thud in response to the smile she flashed at him, Finn set Josh gently on the mat on the floor and thought that the least said about that particular organ, beating, thudding, lurching or doing anything else for that matter, the better.

The following morning, Georgie stepped through the front door of the apartment and dropped her bag on the console table. The therapy session she'd just had had been a mixed bag, as indeed had the last twenty-four hours.

On the one hand, as she'd told the therapist, she was now glad Finn had made her tell him some of what had happened to her. If she did inevitably have the odd day when things got a bit much, and her anxieties descended, it would come as no surprise to anyone, which in turn would ease some of the stress of it.

Furthermore, she'd discovered that a problem shared was literally a problem halved. Not that Josh was a problem, of course, but undoubtedly, on a practical level at least, parenting with Finn was a whole lot easier than doing it on her own. She hadn't realised how much she'd relied on the support of other people when she and Josh had been in hospital or how stressful she'd found having to be constantly on the alert without it.

And, although it was early days and she couldn't be certain the novelty might not wear off, Finn certainly seemed to be reliable. Last night he'd told her he'd take the night shift, since a grizzly Josh had a tooth coming through, and this morning at dawn she'd gone through to the nursery to find him sprawled in a chair with their son, arms out, draped across his chest, both fast asleep. One big hand had lain splayed on Josh's back, protective, warm and secure, and the sight had melted her heart.

However, warring with the feelings of relief, gratitude and warmth were the resentment and jealousy that she'd experienced over breakfast yesterday and which hadn't entirely ebbed. To her shame, despite Finn's generosity and support, she'd been relieved to see his initial uncertainty and clumsiness when left on his own to deal with the messier side of parenting. Not that it had lasted for long. His natural competence had soon risen to the challenge, and watching him interact with Josh subsequently, his ease and instant adoration highlighting her own failings, was like a twist of the knife in her chest, every single time.

Such as now, she thought, coming to an abrupt halt in the doorway to the sitting room, her breath catching in her throat. Finn and Josh were lying on their fronts on the floor, nose to nose. Josh was grabbing at Finn's mouth, giggling and squealing while Finn, resting his chin on his hands, was patiently letting him, simply staring back at him in awe.

She ought to be glad that he'd taken to fatherhood so well, she knew, taking in the scene and feeling an ache throb deep within her. She ought to be relieved that he seemed to be taking his responsibilities so seriously. She shouldn't be jealous of a connection that was instant and deep. She shouldn't feel bitter about the fact that it was a connection she'd been denied. She should be glad that Finn looked to be taking an approach to parenthood that was so different to her own experience.

She was all that, and she wished she could shake off the negativity and focus on the positives, but she couldn't and she lived in fear that at any moment the ugly emotions swirling around inside her would rise up and make her say or do something she might regret.

'How did it go?' he asked, glancing up at her, his eyebrows raised.

'All good.'

'Come and join us.'

She gathered her hair up and gave it a quick twist, then with a small smile shook her head. 'Maybe later.'

CHAPTER FIVE

THE ARRIVAL OF the nanny went some way to easing the volatility of Georgie's emotions. Mrs Gardiner was a sensible woman of sixty with decades of experience and spot-on instincts, whom Josh adored. Discreet, non-interfering and non-judgemental, she knew exactly when to step in with a subtle suggestion and when to back off and leave Georgie to it.

As the days passed and they settled into a rhythm, Georgie's strength and well-being improved. Her belief in herself and her confidence grew, and gradually her insecurities and doubts lessened. The more she saw how Finn's continuing interest and involvement benefited their son, the less she saw him as a threat, and her resentment and jealousy started to fade.

Unfortunately, with this progress came a growing awareness of Finn not just as a father but as a man, a man with whom she'd once burned up the sheets. The excruciating moment she'd barged into his bedroom was becoming harder to forget. The dreams she'd had immediately afterwards were getting worse and more lurid in their detail, and now, alarmingly, during the day too the image of him standing there in just a towel, wet and semi-naked, kept popping into her head, sending her temperature soaring and stealing her breath.

That he was gorgeous went without saying, and it was true that she'd developed something of an obsession with his strong and capable hands that had once been so hot and skilful on her body but were now so infinitely careful and gentle when handling Josh. But it was more than his many physical attractions that tugged at something deep inside her. It was his endless patience, the wholehearted attention he paid Josh and his rock-solid dependability. His self-confidence and reassuring air of authority. For a girl who'd had none of that growing up, these traits of his were incredibly appealing.

As a whole, Finn was heady stuff and she found it all very confusing. She'd become increasingly tongue-tied around him and went bright red whenever she did manage to hold any sort of conversation with him, and it was a mortifying state of affairs because she'd never been the bashful sort.

It was therefore a good thing that in the evenings, once Josh had gone to sleep, Finn disappeared to catch up on work. At least she was spared agonising small talk over supper while trying to sort out how she felt about everything and trying not to remember the things they'd once done together, even if they probably did need to get to know one another better on a level other than the carnal.

However, things would settle down soon enough, she reminded herself for the hundredth time as she navigated the pushchair into the café where she'd arranged to meet Carla for an impromptu weekday lunch a week later. It was a period of adjustment, that was all.

And once they had adjusted she and Finn would discuss how to move forwards. Even though he'd already told her that he'd take care of both her and Josh financially, which was one less thing to have to worry about, at some point in the not-too-distant future she'd have to dip her toe back into the world of work and see if anyone would employ her. She'd loved her job. She couldn't imagine not ever working again. Mrs Gardiner had said she would stay as long as she was needed, so maybe she'd even go with them when Georgie and Josh eventually moved out of the penthouse and set up home somewhere conveniently near by.

Spying Carla sitting at a table in the corner that had plenty of space for a pushchair beside it and feeling a grin spread across her face, Georgie made her way over.

'Hi!' she said, giving Carla, who stood up, a quick kiss on the cheek.

'Wow, you look better,' said her friend with a smile.

'I feel better,' Georgie replied, taking off her coat

and sitting down. In honour of the outing she'd styled her hair for the first time in months and slapped on some make-up. This morning she'd looked at herself in the mirror and noticed with delight that the colour had returned to her cheeks and her eyes had regained the sparkle she'd missed so much. 'Practically back to normal.'

'Hotel penthouse life is clearly suiting you.'

'It is. I don't have to lift a finger, so I'm getting plenty of rest. Finn has food sent up and it's so delicious I've put on a stone.'

'You needed to.'

Georgie grinned. 'I know.'

'Any regrets?'

Only that she turned into an awkward teen with a crush whenever Finn was around. 'None at all.'

'I'm glad.'

'So am I.'

'And how's my gorgeous little boy?'

'Thriving.'

'Can I have a cuddle?'

'Of course.' Reaching down, Georgie unstrapped Josh, eased him out of the pushchair and handed him over. 'How was your trip?' she asked, watching as her son tried to grab Carla's necklace and feeling her heart squeeze when he giggled.

'Good,' said Carla, taking his chubby little hand and wiggling it instead. 'Exhausting. The usual obstacles to overcome but nothing I couldn't handle.

Far more interestingly, how's your hot baby-daddy flatmate?'

Eeew. 'Please don't ever refer to him like that again.'

Carla grinned. 'Is he as gorgeous as you remember?'

Every bit of it. And much more so now she'd caught glimpses of the man beneath the very attractive surface. 'Yup,' she said, automatically thinking about him in a towel and inevitably, irritatingly, feeling herself blush.

'Aha!' said Carla, who was extremely perceptive and knew her way too well. 'Intriguing. I sense a story. Once we've ordered, you need to tell me absolutely *everything.*'

Where the hell were they?

Listening to Georgie's voicemail recording click in for the dozenth time, Finn hung up and tossed his phone onto the buttoned ottoman that had once remained uncluttered but now served as a general dumping ground for things that hadn't existed in his life pre-Georgie and Josh.

He'd arrived home half an hour ago after a lengthy meeting, expecting to be greeted by the noise and activity that over the last two weeks he'd become used to, and that unexpectedly he'd begun to welcome, in fact, since it provided a distraction to the continued lack of progress the investigation agency was making in locating his real parents.

Instead, he'd been met with silence. Georgie hadn't left a note and she wasn't answering her phone, and it was Mrs Gardiner's day off. He had no idea where anyone was, and he didn't like it. He didn't like it one little bit, not least because it had just occurred to him that Georgie could waltz out of here taking Josh with her at any point. In fact, he thought as his pulse skipped a beat and he suddenly went icy cold, she could well have already done so.

When they'd first moved in she'd badly needed his support. She'd been in no fit state to take control and only too happy to let him dictate what was going to happen. Now, however, she was stronger, fitter. He'd watched the transformation happen—the hollows in her cheeks slowly filling out, a healthy pink replacing the grey tinge to her skin. He'd witnessed with a strange sort of pride her increased confidence and the growing ease with which she interacted with their son.

In response to the way she'd blossomed, he'd experienced an annoying and frustrating surge in attraction, which he had no hope of assuaging, since not only was she still incredibly vulnerable, but it was also blindingly obvious that she had absolutely no desire to explore the possibility that the chemistry that had once consumed them still existed. She could barely even look at him and when she did she clearly found it uncomfortable, which was why he absented himself every evening. He claimed he had to work, but he didn't because, despite being in total control of his company for the last thirteen years or so, he'd recently discovered that he had no problem with delegation.

Instead he spent the time in the basement of the hotel, either whipping up a storm in the gym or ploughing up and down the pool to ease the need and frustration pummelling through him. How could she not share the attraction he felt so strongly? he found himself wondering. Exactly how fragile was she still? And then, why the hell couldn't he seem to stop thinking about his son in relation to his father?

The longer he spent with Josh, the greater the connection that built and the deeper the fascination that grew, the more he regretted the fact that the two had never had the chance to meet. Would his father's illness have been easier for them both to handle if they'd known about Josh? Would it have brought happiness? Would it have bought them both more time? It was a regret that was irrational and made no sense. His so-called father deserved no sympathy and no forgiveness. Yet that didn't stop the insidious wistfulness creeping into his head and taking root.

Frustratingly, no amount of exercise seemed to clear his head or calm his body, and Georgie's unexplained absence this afternoon was making things worse. Although he could work out from the fact that nothing seemed to have been taken that she probably *hadn't* gone for good, as she got even better there'd be less keeping her here, and that was a concern.

He wasn't losing Josh, he thought with a touch of

grim desperation as he stalked into the kitchen to make himself some coffee. Not now. Not ever. He was loving the time they were spending together getting to know each other. He found him utterly intriguing and was continually staggered by the depth of the bond he shared with this tiny person, for whom he would willingly die.

Yet how could he stop Georgie from walking out and taking Josh with her? With what she'd been through he had some leverage but using it did *not* appeal. The legal route would take months. Realistically, there was nothing he could do.

Unless…

He froze suddenly, his pulse racing and his head spinning.

There was one way. A bit dramatic possibly, but, without doubt, binding.

Commitment had never held any interest for him before. He'd witnessed Jim's grief when Alice had died, all the more potent for his restraint, as well as the lingering sadness that had tinged his life for the remaining twenty years he'd had of it. Finn had no desire to experience any of that for himself, regardless of the examples of happiness set by the one or two of his friends who had married. To date he'd never met anyone who'd threatened the status quo and right now, with the frustration and confusion he felt over his identity, he was not in any position to enter into a relationship with anyone.

Apart from his son.

During the two months following Jim's death, he'd found himself dwelling increasingly on the idea of love and what it meant, and finding it tainted because surely lying and betrayal formed no part of it. But Josh had made him reconsider. The strength of his feelings for this tiny person, *his* tiny person, blew him away. He was *not* losing him and he was *not* having Josh growing up not knowing him. So if hitching himself to Georgie was the price he had to pay to secure Josh then that was what he'd do and to hell with the X-rated dreams it might give him and the additional discomfort it would no doubt cause her.

His swift but absolutely right decision had nothing whatsoever to do with a subconscious desire to create the family that deep down he might possibly crave. Or the fact that he'd got used to having them around and couldn't stomach the thought of the silence and emptiness their absence would bring. And of course he wasn't worried about abandonment and rejection and being left all alone again. What he'd come up with was a purely practical solution to an unthinkable possibility and a means to eliminating a very great risk, and he'd implement it just as soon as she turned up.

Which, *finally*, he thought darkly as he heard the sound of the front door opening and closing and abandoned the coffee to stride towards it, was now.

'Where have you been?' he said curtly, relief, a shot of unwanted desire and something else undefinable making him sound short.

Having parked the pushchair just inside the door, Georgie glanced up at him, her eyebrows raised no doubt in response to his tone. 'Out,' she said, turning her attention to Josh, unbuckling him and lifting him free.

'Where?'

'We had lunch with Carla.'

'I called.'

'My phone ran out of battery.'

'It's late.'

'We were chatting. I lost track of time.'

'You should have left a note.'

As she fitted Josh to her hip, she turned to him, her eyes narrowing minutely and her chin jutting up. 'Are you implying I'm somehow accountable to you, Finn?'

No. Yes. Dammit. 'No.'

'So why are you so cross?'

'You weren't here when I got home. That's never happened before. I was worried.'

She froze, tension suddenly pouring off her as the colour bled from her face. 'Josh is fine,' she said, her voice tight. 'Truly. Look.'

What? No. She couldn't believe that he'd think she'd hurt him, could she? Hell, just how bad had things got? 'That wasn't what I meant at all.'

'Really?'

'No,' he said with a decisive shake of his head.

'Then what did you mean?'

There was no way he could explain the emotions

that had ripped through him when it had occurred to him that she and Josh might have gone for good. He wasn't entirely sure he fully understood them himself. Perhaps it would be best to get to the point. 'I have a proposal.'

Her gaze turned quizzical, wary. 'What kind of a proposal?'

'A way forward that will suit us all. Permanently.'

She frowned. 'By "proposal" you don't mean marriage, do you?'

'No.'

'Phew. Thank goodness for that.'

'I wouldn't go thanking goodness just yet.'

'Why not?'

'Because instead, you and I are going to enter into a civil partnership.'

If Georgie hadn't been holding on quite so tightly to Josh she might well have dropped him in shock. A civil partnership? Was Finn being serious? He couldn't be. And yet he didn't look as if he was joking. His jaw was set and he wasn't smiling. His gaze was fixed on hers with an intensity that was both unnerving and oddly exciting. He clearly meant every word.

'What on earth makes you think *that's* a good idea?' she asked, ignoring the little leap of her pulse and concentrating on the fact that a civil partnership may not technically be marriage but it was just as much of a commitment and equally unnecessary.

'It will provide security for Josh.'

Not 'would' but 'will', she noticed. So this wasn't a hypothetical proposal. Finn had given it quite a bit of thought already and evidently considered it a fait accompli. Too bad for him that she didn't. 'He already has security without it,' she pointed out. 'We've added your name to his birth certificate and he now carries your surname instead of mine. Plus financially you've set him up for life.'

'That's not enough.'

Of course it was enough. It was more than enough. So what was going on? What more security could Josh have or need? Unless it wasn't only Josh Finn was thinking of. 'Is this in some way about you?' she asked, since there was absolutely no chance it was about her.

Something flickered in the depths of his eyes, something that suggested she'd hit the nail on the head. 'Why would it be about me?'

Hmm. 'You do know that I have no intention of ever preventing Josh from seeing you or vice versa, don't you? Even if I wanted to, which I don't, I don't see how it would be possible.'

'I have no doubt you mean that at the moment.'

Ouch. 'Don't you trust me?'

'It's early days.'

'I'm well aware of that,' she said coolly, still stinging at the realisation he didn't see her progress in the same light as she did.

'Then you'll understand why a formal arrangement is necessary.'

'I can understand why you think it might be, but I don't agree.'

'It will benefit you, too.'

Oh? 'In what way?' she asked, transferring Josh to the other hip.

'Commit to me and you'll have the stability you admitted you need. You'll never want for anything again.'

Well, materially that might be true, yet he'd promised her that already. And what about him? What advantages would it have for him? Was he somehow hoping for a friends-with-benefits sort of thing? He'd better not be. 'What would you get from it?'

'Peace of mind.'

'Anything else?'

'No.'

Right. So not sex. Obviously. Stupid of her. Why would she even have thought it when he showed absolutely no interest in her like that? Damn those scorchingly hot dreams she'd been having about him.

'What would happen if either of us met someone else?' she asked, thinking that, while she couldn't imagine ever doing so herself, Finn was gorgeous and a billionaire and presumably had women flinging themselves at him left, right and centre. She'd seen zero evidence of it to date, but that could well change once things settled down.

'We'll cross that bridge if and when we come to

it,' he said, which wasn't exactly a denial. 'Think about it, Georgie. What do you have to lose?'

The hint of arrogance and condescension in Finn's voice annoyed her even more than the tiny irrational stab of jealousy she felt at the thought of him with another woman, but actually none of this was about her, was it? This was about Josh. Too much of his short life had been taken up with her illness and she owed it to him to make amends. Goodness knew she hadn't been the best of mothers. In fact, she must have been among the worst.

Surely he'd be better off with two parents together. Didn't the statistics suggest precisely that? The inconvenient and all-consuming attraction she felt for Finn would fade to a manageable level eventually. It already had done a bit. Look at the way the shock of his suggestion had rid her of her ridiculous embarrassment around him.

And they were hardly strangers any more. She'd even go so far as to say that they had a weird kind of connection that had nothing to do with Josh, an odd sense of recognition that made her think 'oh, that's right, it's you', which she'd felt the night they'd met, and which hit her with increasing regularity now.

And really, how bad would such a situation be for her? she thought, on one hand barely able to believe that she was even considering Finn's preposterous suggestion yet on the other totally seeing the sense of it. They got on well enough. And he was right. She *would* have the stable family unit she'd always yearned for, along with the security that Finn could provide.

If they were joined in partnership he wouldn't be able to just get up and leave, would he? Should she have a relapse he wouldn't abandon Josh, and therefore he wouldn't abandon *her*. They'd be safe. He'd told her she'd always have his support, which she believed, and she wasn't going to get anything like it anywhere else. She wasn't exactly an attractive prospect and it wasn't as if there was anyone else waiting in the wings.

Ultimately, despite his arrogance and condescension, Finn had a point. She really did have nothing to lose. In fact, she had everything to gain, and so, to ensure the best future for Josh in particular, it really was a no-brainer.

'All right,' she said with a brief nod. 'If it's a civil partnership you want, it's a civil partnership you shall have.'

CHAPTER SIX

THE CEREMONY TOOK place in a register office a stone's throw from Finn's hotel a week later, the usual lengthy bureaucracy associated with such an event magically disappearing the moment he produced an enormous cheque, which only went to demonstrate yet again that once he wanted something he didn't stop until he got it.

The arrangements hadn't been complicated in any case. Georgie had only wanted Carla there, and, apart from their son, Finn had no relations. His mother had been hit by a bus when he was ten, he'd told her, his father had died of terminal cancer around three months ago, and he had no siblings. He was as alone in this world as she was, and when she'd discovered this she'd had the fanciful notion that by hitching her wagon to his she might be rescuing him as much as he'd rescued her.

Faintly unsettled by that thought and unwilling to acknowledge what the accompanying squeeze of her heart might mean, Georgie had joked that it was going to be a small ceremony, and indeed it was. She wore a knee-length ivory dress and matching coat. Finn had on a dark suit that fitted as if made for him, which it probably was, and a snowy white shirt open at the collar that drew attention to the firmness of his jaw and strong planes of his face.

She didn't know quite why they'd dressed up. There was nothing remotely weddingy or romantic about either the venue or the occasion. But that didn't douse the flicker of warmth that uncurled deep within her when they stood together with a thankfully beautifully behaved Josh in Finn's arms while Mrs Gardiner, who'd doubled up as the second witness, took the photo she'd insisted on taking after they'd all signed the register. Nor did it stop her noticing how smoulderingly hot her new… What? Not husband… So partner…? How smoulderingly hot he looked and how delicious he smelled close up.

Not that any of that mattered, any more than the weird idea that the ceremony was somehow special did. She'd get over that nonsense. Nothing had changed. And, while the way Finn made her physically feel was going to continue to be hard to ignore, it wasn't impossible. She was made of stern stuff. If she could get through the insanely tough initial stages of post-partum psychosis, she could handle this inconvenient attraction, however insistent. It wasn't as if there was any other option when how she felt was so clearly one-sided. She was hardly going to throw herself at him and suggest a repeat of that wild night they'd spent together. Heaven forbid. His likely rejection would be mortifying.

However, for the sake of their son, she and Finn could be perfectly civil and mature about all of this, and she, at least, intended to start with the lunch they were about to embark upon to mark the occasion. Carla had gone straight back to work after the ceremony and Mrs Gardiner had taken Josh back to the apartment for his customary nap, which left her and Finn in one of the many restaurants in his company's portfolio, together and on their own for the first time in weeks.

'What shall we toast to?' she asked, once they'd sat down at their table and a bottle of champagne had been delivered and poured.

Finn arched one dark eyebrow. 'Is there any need to toast anything?'

'I think so… Ooh, I know. How about to no longer being alone?'

He didn't say anything, merely carried on looking at her steadily, his gaze unwavering and unfathomable, and for one horrible moment she thought she'd got it all wrong. But just as she was beginning to feel a bit of a fool sitting there with her hand outstretched, he touched his glass to hers and gave her the faintest of smiles before lifting the glass to his lips and tipping half of its contents down his throat.

'So why didn't you want any of your friends to be a witness?' she said, taking a sip of her own drink and for some reason feeling ridiculously pleased that she hadn't got it wrong after all. 'Come to think of it, do you *have* any friends?' She hadn't heard any mention of any.

'Of course I do,' he said, setting his glass down and twirling the stem between his fingers and thumb. 'One of them's on honeymoon, and it didn't seem worth bothering any of the others for something that was merely a formality.'

Oh. Right. Well. That told her. Just as well she hadn't been harbouring any ideas of their civil partnership being anything other than purely practical.

'Do they know about me and Josh?' she asked, slightly distracted by the mesmerising movement of his fingers, as so often happened whenever she looked at his hands.

'If they do it'll have been via the press.'

So he wasn't exactly shouting the news of their union from the rooftops. Which was fine. There was absolutely no reason why he should, she told herself, lifting her gaze and getting a grip. 'Will I ever meet any of them?'

'I imagine so.'

'I look forward to it,' she said, realising with some surprise that it was true. She wanted to know more about this man and, weirdly, not just because he was the father of her child.

'Why didn't you want your parents there today?'

With a jolt she refocused and, as usual whenever she thought of her parents, a tight knot of anger and resentment and God only knew what else formed in her stomach. 'There wouldn't have been any point,' she said, hearing the faint note of bitterness in her voice and inwardly cringing. 'They wouldn't have come even if we had been on speaking terms. Marriage and civil partnerships are far too conventional for their way of life.'

'You mentioned they live in a commune.'

'That's right. They do.'

'Where?'

'I have no idea. They travel around. They always have.'

'Even when you were young?'

'Even then.'

'What was it like?'

'Great in some ways, awful in others,' she said with a casual shrug designed to hide the strange combination of pain and happiness that accompanied memories of her childhood. 'When I was very young, not having to go to school was fantastic. I had no set bedtimes and I could eat what I liked, although, since we only really had lentils and vegetables, I guess that wasn't such a luxury. The first time I had a grilled tuna steak I thought I'd died and gone to heaven. It's still my favourite thing to eat. Anyway, there were no boundaries and zero discipline. In hindsight, I must have been totally feral. We all were, really.'

'All?'

'Wherever we lived and however many families we lived with, there were always *lots* of children.'

'It sounds idyllic.'

'I know,' she said, considering it from the point of view of growing up with only one parent and no siblings. 'But it wasn't.' Not for her, and definitely not for Carla. 'Not for a teenager, at least.'

'Why not?'

She frowned for a moment. 'I think subconsciously I really needed those boundaries to prove that I mattered. That my parents did actually care about me. And because I didn't have any, I went looking for them.'

'How?'

'I became a classic attention-seeking teen. I used to dress up and hang out in bars and order drinks while underage and flirt with all sorts of inappropriate people, desperate for someone to come and haul me home and ground me after some stern words.'

'And did they?'

'Nope,' she said with a sigh of the deep disappointment that annoyingly she still couldn't seem to shake even now, a decade later. 'Never. Once I got caught shoplifting and was delivered home by the owner of the shop with a warning and the only thing my parents were cross about was that the face cream I'd nicked wasn't organic. Eventually I figured that the only person who was going to look out for me was me and so I decided to take control of my own life. I managed to blag my way into a sixth-form college and then got into university. As if that wasn't conventional enough, I became a lawyer, at which point my parents pretty much disowned me. We haven't been properly in touch much since.'

'Do you miss them?'

She stared at him, for a moment completely taken aback. What an odd question. She'd never thought about it like that. She'd always been too stuck in a rut of simmering resentment and disappointment to allow herself to grieve for the loss of what could have been.

'I think I miss the *idea* of them,' she said after a few moments of consideration. 'I envy families. I never really had a proper one. The commune was no substitute. I was angry with my parents for a long time. Maybe I still am a bit. They let me down in every way possible. They failed at everything. No child deserves to feel unloved and unwanted. They should have been responsible. They should have been *better*. It's kind of in the job description.'

A job description that was hers now, she thought, making a silent promise to be the best parent she could for Josh. She might not have got off to a good start on the motherhood front but she would now do everything in her power to prevent her son *ever* feeling the way she had. Josh would never have to question whether he mattered. Whether he was truly loved. He'd never feel he had to find support else-where. He would never have to seek the attention he craved by hitting bars and clubs and engaging in unsuitable flirting.

'Do they know you've been ill?'

She shook her head. 'I didn't see the point of telling them. They wouldn't have been any help. They'd have just boiled up some hemp and sung a song or something. They've had the luxury of never being properly ill. At least, as far as I'm aware.'

'Have you told them about Josh?'

'I emailed my mother and got a reply warning me about the dangers of disposable nappies.'

'Their loss.'

And so it was, she realised as those two simple words sliced through the complex emotions she felt about her upbringing and pulverised the resentment and the pain. Finn was right. Her parents would never know her or him and they would never know their grandson, and that *was* their loss.

It wasn't her fault that they'd been so undeserving of the role. However much she might have wondered over the years what she'd done wrong or what she could have done differently, the answer to that was nothing. The responsibility for her well-being had been entirely theirs.

Well, she was done with them and with looking back. She had to look forward. Her family was Josh now. Maybe even Finn too, who was perceptive and clever, who'd just shone a spotlight on the knotted mess of emotion she'd lived with for years and unravelled it in an instant and who was not a man to be underestimated. In any department.

Feeling strangely lightheaded while at the same time all warm and fuzzy, Georgie sat back and watched as he drained his glass, her gaze snagging on the strong column of his throat and the tantalising wedge of flesh that his open-necked shirt revealed.

'So what was growing up like for you?' she asked with a touch of huskiness that she cleared with a tiny cough. 'It must have been tough not having a mother around.'

As he lowered his glass she saw a shadow pass over his face and a flash of bleakness in the depths of his eyes. 'It wasn't the easiest of times.'

'Before that?'

'I don't really remember.'

'How did your father cope?'

'As well as could be expected.'

'Do you want to talk about it?'

'I'd rather not.'

Fair enough. She was more than happy to back off. The afternoon was far too sunny for such sombre conversation and there was no need to push a topic that was clearly off limits. She and Finn had plenty of time to talk about histories and dreams. Years, in fact, she thought, the reality of what she'd agreed to hitting her suddenly and making her head swim for a moment. 'Will you tell me about your business, then?'

'Which bit of it?'

'Well, how did it come about?' she asked, thinking that, honestly, getting him to open up was like trying to get blood from a stone.

'When I was eighteen and had left school I started working behind the bar of a club in the centre of the city.'

'I bet you were good at it.' With his darkly devastating looks and brooding charisma she had no doubt that people—well, women mainly—would have been tripping over themselves to be served by him.

'I was,' he said with the glimmer of a smile, the tension she could see gripping his shoulders easing a little. 'I was very good at it. And more importantly I got a massive kick out of it.'

'You didn't want to go to university?'

'I had a place at Oxford to read Maths but I gave it up.'

'That was brave.' University for her had been a lifeline and she'd loved it.

'It was the arrogance of youth.'

'Which in your case was justified.'

'So it turned out. Six months later the club had become a go-to destination and hit all the A-lists. Soon after that the manager, who also owned it, fell ill. He had to take some time off and I stepped in. I started doing the books, figured out where savings could be made and margins improved, and wound up increasing the profits by fifty per cent. When it eventually came up for sale I bought it. I worked bloody hard and I expanded and diversified and things went from there.'

Admiration and awe surged through her. 'And you did it all on your own.'

'With the support of my father,' he said, his mouth twisting slightly as his smile faded. 'He lent me the money to buy the club in the first place, and gave me endless advice. He was an accountant and very shrewd.'

'You must miss him.'

He didn't answer, just looked so tortured for a moment that it tugged on her heartstrings. 'Was it quick?'

'It took around a year,' he said, his voice oddly flat. 'I received his diagnosis the night you and I met.'

She gave a slow nod of understanding. 'That was why you looked so sad.'

'Did I?'

'Well, desolate really.'

'I was drowning my sorrows.'

'And then I rocked up and intruded. Sorry about that.'

'Don't be,' he said. 'You were the perfect distraction.'

Her breath caught and a hot shiver ran through her. 'You were the perfect birthday present,' she said huskily. 'It was a good night.'

'It was better than good.'

His dark, glittering gaze remained locked onto

hers and scorchingly vivid memories suddenly poured into her head. The air surrounding her thickened. The hustle and bustle of the restaurant faded. Up until this point she hadn't realised how much of a chaperone, a shield, Josh had been. Without him, she felt wild and carefree and she suddenly wanted to stand up and lean over and kiss the man sitting opposite her looking at her so intently. Her mouth was dry and her heart was pounding, and deep inside she ached. She wanted to grab his hand and take him home and have him seduce the hell out of her all over again.

But none of that would happen. It couldn't, even if the heat and desire *had* been mutual, which it clearly wasn't. What with the risk of pregnancy and the chance that it might induce another psychotic episode, she was never having sex again. It was vaguely ironic that her libido had returned when it was of least use but she had to ignore it. Starting now, she thought, shifting to alleviate the ache only to accidentally knock his knee with hers and jolt as though electrocuted.

'Sorry,' she muttered, blushing fiercely while mentally throwing her hands up in despair.

'No problem,' Finn replied, unlike her, completely unmoved by the moment, if the inscrutability of his expression was anything to go by. 'We should order.'

Despite appearances, Finn was anything but unmoved by his brand-new civil partner. Theoretically, the ceremony should have changed nothing. The whole event had been a legal and bureaucratic process designed to bind Josh to him permanently, and that was it. He hadn't given Georgie a ring or planned a honeymoon and the lunch they'd had afterwards had hardly been a celebration.

However, for some baffling reason things *had* changed. A week in and there now seemed to be an inexplicable intimacy about living with her that somehow hadn't existed before. At night he'd started imagining her in bed and what he might do to her should he find himself ever in it with her. In the mornings, when he heard the sound of the shower running, he now envisaged her in it, wet and naked.

He seemed attuned to her every movement. Her scent lingered even when she wasn't around. When home, she'd taken to wandering around the apartment in tiny shorts and T-shirts that drew his gaze to her long legs and spectacularly returning curves. When going out she did at least put on proper clothes, none of which were either particularly tight or revealing, but that didn't provide much relief. He knew what lay underneath regardless, and to his immense irritation he couldn't stop thinking about it.

And then there were the little things that he'd noticed and now couldn't un-notice, such as her habit of nibbling the end of the pen that she used when writing in her diary. The extraordinarily expressive delight with which she savoured the food she ate. The way she gathered her hair up and then with a sort of flick of her fingers twisted it once before letting it go.

He couldn't stop thinking about *any* of it and he existed in an agonising, limbo-like state of wanting to back her up against a wall and slake his desire yet not being able to do one damn thing about it, of yearning to escape her mind-scrambling orbit but needing to be as close to his son as possible. At least she had no idea of the battle raging inside him. She couldn't. If she did she'd never prance around the place so scantily clad. She wasn't that foolish.

Nevertheless, everything else about the situation was driving him demented, and despite his best efforts to contain it his mood of recent days had not gone unnoticed. From time to time he'd caught her looking at him, her eyes on him searing his skin and burning through him, as if deliberating whether to question him about it.

She was doing it now, sitting out here on the terrace that overlooked London, staring at him from over the rim of the mug she drank coffee out of every morning, which had 'world's sexiest lawyer' emblazoned across it, as if he needed a reminder.

'If you have something to say, just say it,' he snapped, unable to stand the scrutiny and the suspense any longer.

'All right,' she said, putting her mug down. 'I've been thinking. What would you say to spending your evenings up here with me instead of disappearing off to wherever it is you go?'

What? No. No way. He barely trusted himself with her in the presence of their son and Mrs Gardiner in broad daylight. He and Georgie in the evening alone with soft lighting and an even softer sofa was *not* happening. 'Work needs me,' he said, which was a big, fat lie, since the team to which he'd delegated everything was doing just fine.

'It would be good to spend some time together without Josh.'

'Why?'

'There are things we should discuss.'

'Like what?'

'How we move forward.'

'Josh is having a nap. We can discuss that now.'

'He's due to wake up any moment and I'd like to know more about you without distractions.'

That wasn't happening either. Talking about himself wasn't something he was particularly fond of doing at the best of times. Right now it was the last thing he wanted to do. And she *was* the distraction. 'You know everything there is to know.' Everything that was relevant, anyway.

'OK, fine,' she said with an exasperated huff. 'You know what? Forget it. I do think we need to talk about the future, but really, I'd just like the company. It's lonely up here on my own every evening. It's quiet.' She gave a careless shrug. 'I dare say I'll survive, though.'

Well, now, how was he to respond to that? Just when he thought he'd successfully shut her down, along came guilt to hit him in the gut like a ton of bricks. He had no excuse really, and to persist with pretending he did would simply be cruel. He wasn't having her feeling lonely because he had an issue with self-control. He'd just have to cope. Because hadn't he vowed to provide her with what she needed whenever she needed it?

'All right,' he muttered, nevertheless slightly wishing that he had less of a problem with breaking promises. 'I'll make some adjustments.'

'Thank you,' she said with a smile so dazzling that it blinded him to the realisation that she'd got up and was walking over to him.

By the time he did register what she was doing it was too late. Before he could brace himself, she'd come to a stop right in front of him and bent down, her scent and her warmth scrambling his senses. The world skidded to a halt and every inch of him froze. Then she reached out and touched her hand lightly to his head, threading her fingers through his hair, and for one heart-stopping, delirious moment he actually thought that she was going to lean in and kiss him.

'What are you doing?' he said hoarsely, his mouth dry and his body aching unbearably.

'You have a piece of toast in your hair.'

She removed her hand and stepped back and he didn't know whether to be gutted or relieved, what to think or what to do, although breathing would be a good start. Followed by getting the hell out of here before he completely gave in to temptation and turned some of his wilder imaginings into reality.

'Where are you going?' she called as he leapt to his feet and stalked back into the apartment as if he had the hounds of hell at his heels.

'Meeting.'

CHAPTER SEVEN

EYEING FINN WARILY as he paced up and down his sitting room one evening several days later, Georgie frowned. Up until a few days ago she'd thought that everything was going really rather well. He seemed pleased with their civil partnership and, although it was a struggle, she was just about keeping a lid on the attraction that she felt for him. She'd had a slight blip when she'd discovered that he'd added tuna steak to the menu of dishes that continued to be sent up, and gone all breathless and gooey inside at the realisation he'd remembered what she'd told him at that lunch, but she'd recovered well enough. It hadn't meant anything. She needed building up, he'd told her when she'd thanked him. She needed the protein. That was all.

Lately, however, Finn had become weirdly distracted, frequently grumpy and anything but friendly. Physically he was around as much as ever, more so now he spent the evenings with her, but spiritually and emotionally he seemed to be on a whole other planet. He volunteered little in the way of conversation and his answers to her questions were monosyllabic.

The tension that now radiated off him had to come from somewhere and she didn't think it was caused by Josh, since being with him was the only time Finn didn't seem stressed. So maybe it was her, she'd begun to think. Maybe he was more annoyed by her habit of leaving the milk out than she'd realised. Maybe she was doing something else wrong. It wouldn't exactly be a first.

Whatever it was, though, Josh was picking up on it now and she'd had enough.

Closing the journal she filled in nightly, and setting both it and the pen she used on the ottoman, Georgie tracked his restless movements for a moment and then pulled her shoulders back and went for it. 'OK, Finn, what's wrong?'

'Why would anything be wrong?' he said, shooting her a glare, which did rather prove her point.

'You're wearing a permanent scowl these days and you've taken to prowling around the apartment like a caged animal.'

He stopped mid-pace and with what looked like a Herculean effort cleared his expression and shot her a tight smile. 'Everything's fine.'

'Hmm,' she said with a sceptical frown. 'Is it work?'

'No.'

'Is it me and Josh?'

'Why would it be you?'

'I'm very aware that this has all been a huge up-heaval for you. The noise and the mess, I mean. It would be completely understandable if you were finding it hard. Your life has changed immeasurably.'

'That's nothing new.'

Her eyebrows lifted. 'Sorry?'

'Nothing,' he said curtly. 'Everything's fine.'

'Are you sure?'

'Yes.'

'Anything you want to talk about?'

'No.'

In the face of such intransigence Georgie gave up. She could try till she was blue in the face and she wouldn't get anywhere. 'OK,' she said. 'It's your call. I rather feel that if you carry on like this sooner or later you're going to burst a blood vessel, but have it your own way.'

'Have it *my* way?' he said with a bark of humour-less laughter. 'You have no idea.'

'Then tell me.'

She shifted to make herself more comfortable, just in case he did want to talk, and suddenly something inside him seemed to snap.

'All right,' he said, his eyes blazing and his hands curling into fists. 'You're right. There is something.'

'What?'

'Do you think, for once, you could put on a bloody dressing gown?'

And with that he turned on his heel and strode out, leaving Georgie staring after him, reeling and agape.

What on earth...?

What was wrong with what she was wearing? There was nothing immodest about the baggy T-shirt or the board shorts that she had on, yet what he'd just said and the way he'd glowered at her while saying it implied that not only did he consider it to be the skimpiest outfit he'd ever seen but also that it bothered him.

However, why would it? He wasn't affected by her. Unless he was, of course, and that tension he was obviously feeling could actually be some kind of sexual frustration because, contrary to what she'd assumed, he *was* still attracted to her.

But no. He couldn't be. She'd seen no evidence of it. There'd been no long, heated looks, no off-the-charts chemistry and no sizzling subtext to their conversations. If that was the case, surely there'd have been signs...

But maybe there had been, she thought suddenly, her heart quickening as the clouds in her head parted to reveal possibilities that had hitherto been hidden. What if some of the looks Finn had given her over the last few weeks, some of his expressions that she hadn't been able to decipher and some of the strange things he'd done, were in fact cases in point?

Take, for example, the way his gaze dropped to her lips pretty much every time they ate together. She'd always vaguely assumed he'd been staring at a stray crumb or perhaps a bit of parsley stuck between her teeth. But what if instead he'd been bombarded with thoughts of kissing her the way she always thought about kissing him whenever she caught herself looking at his mouth? And what about his habit of taking a step back whenever she approached? Could he be doing that because he found her proximity somehow disturbing?

He appeared to have such a tight grip on his control, but maybe the absence of a reaction hid a very different kind of response. What if when she'd barged in on him that night and found him naked save for a towel he hadn't been as unmoved as he appeared? What if when her knee had brushed against his the day they'd had lunch, he'd been as affected as her? And what if his disappearance every night was less about catching up with work and more about avoiding her?

Or was she seeing signs where there were none?

It was entirely possible, but, if she was right and these were signs that she'd missed, then she was not only an idiot but she was also not as back to her old self as she'd imagined because that Georgie would never have missed anything.

But that wasn't important right now. Assuming she hadn't got things completely wrong, Finn appeared to want her and she might as well admit that she wanted him. She'd tried to ignore it and treat him like a flatmate, as if she were back in her old flat in Kensal Rise that she'd shared with three others, two of whom had been men she'd had no interest in, but that hadn't exactly worked. Despite her best intentions, she hadn't been able to entirely stop fantasising about him naked, about what they might get up to if she should happen to find herself in his vicinity naked too.

So what was going to happen next?

They clearly couldn't carry on like this. Things would eventually come to a head and erupt. And what was she going to do when they did? Well, she was never having sex again obviously, but, assuming Finn was amenable, there was no reason they couldn't do other things. From what she remembered he'd been spectacularly good at those other things and he hadn't exactly complained about her skills either.

Did she have the courage to tell him what she now quite desperately wanted, she wondered, her heart beginning to pound with excitement as her stomach churned nervously. Once upon a time she wouldn't have hesitated, but now... On the other hand, while she *had* been scarred by what had happened to her, it didn't have to define her going forward, did it?

So how hard would it be to go to Finn and tell him what she wanted? All it would take was guts, and heaven knew she had plenty of those. If she tried her hardest and he still sent her away, if she'd read too much into things and got completely the wrong end of the stick, then so be it. After everything she'd been through she could handle a spot of mortification. She could handle anything.

* * *

Cursing himself for what he'd revealed, and deeply regretting his momentary loss of control, Finn stormed into his room and slammed the door. If only Georgie had backed off and left him to stew. Instead she'd pushed and prodded and told him to have it his way, which was an absolute joke since his way involved her being horizontal in his bed, sighing and gasping beneath his hands and mouth, a scenario that wasn't going to happen. As if that wasn't enough she'd then leaned back and lifted her legs to tuck them under her, a movement that made the fabric of her tiny T-shirt tighten enticingly against her breasts, and he'd lost it, any hope he might have had of making it out of there with his pride intact history.

His movements jerky, Finn yanked his T-shirt over his head and tossed it on the bed, only to spin round at the sound of his bedroom door opening. Georgie stood there, silhouetted in the space, and as a bolt of desire shot through him, nearly taking out his knees, he swore beneath his breath.

He should have known she wouldn't let his parting shot go. He should have known she'd follow him. That perhaps he subconsciously *had* known and had wanted her to do so, so that they might continue where they'd left off that first night she'd barged into his room, wasn't something he wanted to contemplate ever. Because if that *did* turn out to be the case it would mean his attempts to get a grip on his unpredictable behaviour had utterly failed.

'What is it with you and knocking?' he said, practically at the end of his tether with his inability to control the futile attraction he felt for her.

'Sorry.'

She stepped forward into the light, into his territory, and he saw that she didn't look sorry. She didn't look sorry in the slightest. 'What do you want?'

'To continue our conversation.'

'We're done.'

'I don't think we are.'

Before he could even think about striding past her and getting the hell out of his room, with its huge bed squatting there like some giant neon sign advertising sex, she'd walked towards him and planted her palms flat on his chest.

'What are you doing?' he said, every muscle in his body freezing while he burned where she touched him.

'I'd have thought it was obvious,' she murmured, moving her hands up over the muscles of his chest while staring at his mouth.

His jaw clenched and his fists tightened. 'I'd advise you to stop.'

'Why?'

Yes, why? his body screamed while his brain fought to be heard. 'Because you're playing with fire.'

'I'm more than happy to be burned.'

'You've been ill.'

'I'm much better now.'

But she still had some way to go. He'd done the research and witnessed her occasional off day. She was by no means totally well yet. 'That's irrelevant.'

'All that's relevant right now is that I want you and you want me.'

Not much point in denying it, really. He needed her so badly he was in physical pain and it was becoming blatantly obvious. Nevertheless...

'What I want doesn't come into it,' he muttered though gritted teeth.

'Yet here we are, all partnered up.'

'For the sake of our son.'

She tilted her head as she lifted her gaze to his, her brown eyes shimmering in the soft light. 'Are you sure about that?'

He had been once. Right now he wasn't sure he could even remember his own name. Her scent and her warmth were destroying his faculties. All he could think of was how good it had been between them and how desperately he wanted to find out if it still could be. 'One hundred per cent.'

'So selfless,' she said with the hint of a smile.

'Don't patronise me.'

'The tension is driving you nuts, isn't it?'

'What tension?' he ground out.

'We could make it go away. *I* could make it go away.'

She ran her hands along his shoulders and down his arms and he shuddered. He had to take a step back, out of her orbit. He had to break the spell she was weaving around him. His thundering heart couldn't take much more and his self-control was fast unravelling. But he couldn't move. His feet appeared to have taken root. And his grip on his sanity, already loosened by weeks of frustration, was slipping away.

'Leave me alone, Georgie,' he said, but the protest was weak and he knew she knew it.

'Give me one last shot and, if you really insist, then I'll go.'

He couldn't speak for trying to drum up the will to insist she leave, regardless of what she did next, and she seemed to take his silence as assent, which maybe it foolishly and recklessly was, because before he knew what she was planning, before he could brace himself for what she might say or do, she'd let go of him, reached down, and gripped the hem of her top.

And as she whipped it off and tossed it to the floor, exposing her lace-covered breasts and inches of beautiful, creamy skin to his ravenous gaze, Finn felt what was left of his resistance crumble and the last remaining vestiges of his self-control shatter.

When, suddenly galvanised into action after minutes of rock-solid stillness, Finn hauled her into his arms and his mouth crashed down on hers, Georgie's first thought was, oh, thank heavens for that. She hadn't known what she would have done next had he rejected her bold move. Back away and flee, most probably, because there was taking a leaf out of his book and not stopping until one got what one wanted, and then there was harassment.

Now, though, as he held her tightly and kissed her as if his life depended on it, she couldn't think at all. Her head was swimming and the electricity zinging through her as a result of his chest hair rubbing against her sensitised skin was enough to power the national grid. She'd forgotten how very good he was at this, how good they were together, and she kissed him back with equal fervour.

When at last Finn lifted his head, his eyes were so dark they were almost black and his breathing was as ragged as hers. 'You really don't play fair,' she heard him murmur harshly over the thunder of her heart.

'You're a hard man to crack.'

'You have no idea how hard I've been.'

She arched her back, pressing her hips more firmly to his, and gave him a quick grin. 'I think I may have some.'

His gaze bored into hers and she shivered. 'Are you sure about this?'

'Yes.'

'What exactly do you want from me?' he persisted.

'Not sex.'

He stilled for a moment and eased back, his expression tortured. 'OK, then,' he said, clearly grappling to contain his surprise and disappointment. 'OK.' And then, hoarsely, 'Out of interest, why not?'

'It's too risky,' she clarified swiftly to put him out of his misery. 'We were careful the last time and look what happened. I can't get pregnant a second time. I can't go through the last six months all over again. Ever. We can do everything else though.'

As her words sank in he shuddered with visible relief. 'Thank God for that.'

'I'm sure you know things I've never even heard of.'

'Based on past experience, I very much doubt that.'

'Is that OK?' she added, suddenly worried that it might not be enough for him.

'I'll take anything you're willing to give.'

Phew. 'Then we're going to be busy.'

'Fine by me.'

He turned with her still in his arms and backed her up towards the bed until her knees hit the edge of it. Together they fell onto the mattress, his hard-muscled weight pinning her down in the most breath-takingly lovely way.

'That's better,' he muttered, lowering his head and capturing her mouth with his in a kiss that blew her mind all over again.

Caught up in a maelstrom of soul-shattering sensation, Georgie gave up thinking and let instinct take over. She lifted her hands to his shoulders, smoothing them over his muscles, feeling them bunch and flex as he held himself off her just enough to prevent crushing her.

He dragged his mouth along her jaw to her ear, nipping at a spot that made her groan as heat sizzled through her, and she gasped, 'You remembered.'

'I remember everything.'

Shifting slightly onto his side, Finn put one large, warm hand on her waist, making her jump and shudder, and then slid it behind her back to unclip her bra. After slipping it off her and throwing it aside he cupped her breast, and with a soft moan she instinctively arched her back to press herself further into his hand. He bent his head and caught one tight nipple between his lips and she whimpered as sparks shot through her. Her hands tightened in his hair, although whether to hold him still or push him lower she couldn't tell. She didn't want the exquisite torment he was subjecting her to to stop but on the other hand she wanted that clever mouth of his all over her. It was the most delicious of dilemmas.

Abandoning her breast, he slid his hand lower, easing beneath the waistband of her shorts and knickers, and she lifted her hips to help him push them down.

'Beautiful,' he muttered gruffly, his gaze singeing her skin as he moved his hand back up her calf, her knee, her thigh, taking his time and lingering in places that had her quivering. When he reached the juncture of her thighs and covered her where she was so hot and needy she cried out. He parted her with his fingers and stroked, and jolts of excitement streaked through her. Her breath caught and her heart thundered and when she reached down to touch him through his jeans his breath shot out in one long hiss.

Unable to lie there impassively while Finn was still partly clothed and doing everything, and desperately wanting to feel him without denim between them, she nudged him to encourage him to roll over, but he stopped her.

'No,' he said roughly, his entire body vibrating with tension. 'You're first.'

Noble, she thought with a shudder at the thought of the pleasure to come. But no. That wasn't happening. Not when she owed him for the whipping-her-top-off moment. 'Who said we have to take turns?'

He went still for a moment and then his eyes darkened and his mouth curved into a slow, smouldering smile. 'Good point.'

He flipped onto his back, taking her with him, and she wriggled down his body. Her hands were trembling as she unbuckled his belt, so much so that she couldn't actually undo the buttons of his fly. He batted her aside to do it himself and the sight of his capable hands with their strong fingers that could cause so much devastation within her liquefied her stomach.

He kicked off his jeans and shorts and then planted his hands on her waist to manoeuvre her into a position in which she was facing his feet and he was gripping her hips and lifting her to where he wanted her and where she wanted to be. Supporting herself on her elbows, she wrapped her fingers around his long, thick, hard length and heard him groan, and then gave a reciprocal one of her own when his tongue touched her sensitive flesh and sent sensation coursing through her.

As she moved her hand up and down the velvety steel of him, and he found her clitoris and licked, her eyelids fluttered shut, her entire body filling with molten heat. She was shaking all over, but not nearly as much as he was when she took him into her mouth. When she started moving her head he moaned against her, and the vibrations sent tiny shock waves shooting through her.

His response stoked hers, making her move faster, which drove him to increase the pressure and the intensity of what he was doing to her and she was fast spiralling out of control. She could feel the tension building inside her, the heat and pleasure winding tight and scrambling her senses, and she seemed to be in synch with him because he was now shifting his hips and thrusting into her mouth as she moved, and his breathing was hot and ragged against her.

Desire soared within her, igniting a desperate ache, and she was just about to reach a hand down to where his tongue was buried to hurry him along, when, as if able to read her mind, he held her still and thrust two fingers inside her and curled them so that they hit that exact spot, and that was it. She flew apart, her orgasm crashing into her, a white-hot burst of pleasure spinning through her like a Catherine wheel. And as stars whirled round her head she took him deep, and with a harsh groan he grabbed her head, tensed and then pulsated hard, spilling into her mouth until neither of them had anything left.

Feeling utterly drained, Georgie eased herself off him and flopped back, lying top to tail against him while waiting for her heartbeat to regulate.

'God, we're good at this,' she said when she had enough breath to speak.

Finn rolled onto his side, and regarded her, his gaze dark and glittering and his face flushed. 'Just think how much better we could be with a bit of practice.'

A sharp shiver raced through her, electrifying her nerve endings all over again. 'I don't know if I'd survive.'

The smile he gave her was slow and full of wicked promise. 'Oh, you'll survive.'

CHAPTER EIGHT

THEY PRACTISED A LOT, and got so good that a week later Georgie thought it was just as well that the walls were soundproofed. Finn was very inventive and, as she'd suspected, he knew things to do with positions and accessories and devices that she'd never even seen before, let alone deployed.

He just had to look at her and she became flushed and aroused. Every night as soon as Josh had been put to bed—indecently soon, actually—Finn took her hand and led her into the nearest bedroom, where they stayed until either day broke or their son woke. She'd lost count of how many orgasms she'd had and she was fast becoming addicted to the things he could do to her.

She wasn't just surviving the way he handled her body, she was thriving on it, as the entries in her diary detailed, which only went to show that oxytocin and dopamine and the endorphins that accompanied them really were good for the brain. And if something was occasionally missing, if she sometimes felt a bit hollow on her way down from the bliss and sort of wished she could have all of him, well, that was the compromise she just had to make, in the same way that all this lovely nocturnal activity came at the cost of the conversation she'd been so keen to encourage.

Her days now had structure and routine and she and Finn were getting on splendidly, and she had absolutely nothing to complain about. However, in the absence of stress and anxiety and sexual frustration, she found that now all she had to wonder about was if and when he was going to introduce her to his friends as promised. He'd shown no indication of it so far, and she couldn't help wondering why not. They were in every night, so it wasn't as if a hectic schedule prevented it. So was it something to do with her, then? With their situation? Or did he see her as unfit for anywhere other than the bedroom?

There was only one way to find out.

'So when am I going to meet your friends?' she asked him one night as they lay sprawled across his enormous bed, the moonlight streaking through the windows and bathing everything in a silvery glow. 'It's been weeks. Are you in some way ashamed of me?'

'What?' he replied, his words muffled by the pillow he'd flopped onto only moments ago. 'Don't be ridiculous.'

Hmm. That wasn't exactly an answer. 'Don't get me wrong,' she said, trying to keep her voice light, 'your attention is very flattering but a girl could get a complex.' Especially a girl like her, with anxieties and insecurities that she knew could pop up at any time.

'She shouldn't.'

'She might.'

He turned his head to the side and levelled her with a long, hot look. 'Really?'

She nodded. 'Really.'

'I'll set something up.'

'Thank you,' she said with a grin.

'You're welcome.'

'I shall cook.'

'There's no need. We'll go out. Or have something sent up.'

'No, I'd like to. I used to love cooking and I can't keep eating all the food the kitchens provide. It's too easy, too convenient and way too delicious. Much more of it and I'll be as big as a house.'

His gaze slowly roamed over her, setting her on fire wherever he let it linger. 'You're fine,' he said, his smile fading and his eyes darkening as he reached for her yet again. 'You're beautiful. And I am in absolutely no way ashamed of you.'

And that was how, the following Friday evening, she and Finn played hosts to his friends, Theo and Kate Knox, and her friend Carla. Finn and Theo had known each other professionally for a couple of years, and socially for one of those, more so since Theo had met Kate and settled down. Kate, his wife of three months, was tall, statuesquely beautiful and heavily pregnant.

Over drinks and nibbles, a starter of salmon and asparagus and a main course of slow-roasted lamb, Georgie listened to the conversation that flowed easily, picking up anything she could about Finn, however tiny, and filing it away for later consideration. She smiled and laughed and made contributions where necessary, but for the most part she found herself surreptitiously watching Kate and trying not to envy her.

The other woman's clear enjoyment of her pregnancy and the serenity and radiance that she emanated were things that had been denied to Georgie, and that filled her with regret and sadness. If only she'd known she was pregnant, things could have been so different. It was hard not to feel cheated.

And then there was the immense love that Kate was lucky enough to bask in. In all honesty Georgie found Theo faintly aloof and more than a bit intimidating, but when he looked at his wife the hard lines of his face softened and the blazing emotion that warmed in his eyes stole her breath. What would it feel like to be on the receiving end of such love and such passion? Would she ever know? It didn't seem likely, given the hand of cards she'd been dealt.

'So how did you and Theo meet?' Carla asked, and Georgie made herself shake off the gloom and focus.

Kate put down her glass of elderflower *pressé*

and gave her husband a look of wry amusement. 'I made myself available on an escort agency website and Theo took against it.'

Goodness, thought Georgie. That she hadn't known.

Theo arched an eyebrow, although a faint smile played at his mouth. 'Indeed,' he said, his dark gaze taking in Finn and Georgie. 'How about you?'

'Georgie picked Finn up in a bar,' Carla said with a wide grin.

'I wouldn't put it quite like that,' Georgie muttered, feeling herself blush.

'Why not?' said Finn, the glance he slid her holding a wicked glint. 'You did.'

'I don't remember you putting up much of a protest.'

'I put up no protest at all.'

'The sparks flying off the two of them could have set fire to a forest,' Carla said, taking a sip of champagne. 'I went up to them to see if Georgie was OK and had to back off for fear of getting singed.'

Oh? 'I don't remember you doing that.'

'I'm not surprised. The fire alarm could have gone off with sprinklers and everything and you'd have been oblivious.'

'And how do you two know each other?' asked Kate, indicating her and Carla.

'Our parents lived on the same commune for a while when we were teenagers,' said Georgie, remembering how excited she'd been at hearing the news of the latest arrivals.

'We clicked instantly,' said Carla. 'Took a few walks together on the wild side. Even after my family moved on we stayed in touch.'

'She's my best friend,' said Georgie.

'Back at you,' said Carla.

'Thank you,' said a suddenly serious Finn to Carla, who, to Georgie's astonishment, blushed.

'You're very welcome.'

'I'll make coffee, shall I?' said Georgie before either of the too-sharp-for-their-own-good Knoxs could voice the curiosity that was filling their expressions.

'I'll help,' said Carla.

Feeling oddly peculiar, Georgie practically ran into the kitchen, with Carla hot on her heels.

'God, Finn really is divine,' said her friend, faux fanning herself with a hand while Georgie turned on the boiling water tap and filled a cafétière. 'All that intensity and focus on you. Blazing. The vibes are extraordinary. Watching you two together *and* Kate and Theo almost makes me want to give up singledom.'

'Finn and I aren't like that, as you know perfectly well,' said Georgie, her chest nevertheless tightening.

'Then what are you like?'

'I'm not entirely sure.'

But she had the suspicion that she knew exactly what she might want it to be like, and she stuck a lid on it because there was absolutely no point chasing rainbows.

And it was a good thing she did too, because it meant that at breakfast a couple of days after the dinner party when Finn made his unexpected announcement she was able to handle it. Josh was squashing a piece of banana between his fingers as he tried to cram it into his mouth. Finn was devouring a croissant and looking so dishevelled and sexy from her early-morning ministrations that Georgie, who was sipping coffee, felt her heart turn over, as it was increasingly wont to do whenever she looked at him.

'I have to go to Paris next weekend,' he said, jolting her out of her reverie and causing the mouthful of coffee she'd just taken to go down the wrong way. 'The Bellevue is finally opening. There's a launch party.'

She coughed and spluttered and banged her chest.

'Are you all right?' he asked with a faint frown of concern.

'Yes,' she said, thumping her chest one last time. 'Fine.'

She was just surprised, that was all. The Bellevue was finished? Well, that was excellent news. She knew a bit from him about how long the works had been going on and how stressful they'd been. She had no reason to feel stung by the fact that Finn had never mentioned the imminent launch of the hotel or the party, a party that must have been planned for weeks, if not months. Or by the lack of an invitation. He owed her nothing. The debt went entirely the other way. She'd be of no benefit to him at such an event anyway.

'When are you going?'

'Saturday.'

In six days. Gutting. Her period was due imminently, which would put a temporary halt to orgasms— for her at least—a halt that would now apparently last longer than she'd hoped. But she'd handle it. It wasn't as if she wouldn't survive without the pleasure he evoked in her. In fact, the delay would make his return all the sweeter.

'That's a shame,' she said, deciding to attribute the disappointment she nevertheless felt to PMT.

'Why?'

'Because I'll miss...'

You.

Well. She certainly wasn't going to tell him that. She'd sound pathetic. Besides, she was already too vulnerable when it came to him. He held all the cards. She held none. So she pulled herself together and lowered her voice, even though Josh was way too young to understand, and finished '...what we've been doing.'

His blue eyes gleamed. 'You don't have to.'

She looked at him quizzically. What did he have in mind? Phone sex? That was something they hadn't tried yet. Could be fun. 'What do you mean?'

'Come with me.'

Her heart skipped a beat and then began to race. 'Really?'

'Why not? Think of it as a belated mini honeymoon.'

Hmm. She'd be better off *not* thinking that actually, since, whatever they were doing, it wasn't romance and she'd be wise not to forget it. 'For how long?'

'A couple of days, maybe three. The party's on the Saturday night and I have some business on the Monday and Tuesday. We'd be back by Tuesday evening at the latest.'

'What about Josh?'

'He can stay here with Mrs Gardiner.'

As usual Finn had all the answers and he made it sound not only easy but also unbelievably tempting. Three days on her own with him in Paris, strolling through the parks and sitting in divine restaurants that had white tablecloths, sparkling crystal and soft, flickering candles...

Or perhaps not, since he'd probably be in meetings most of the time, but whatever. She could see it now—the party, the luxury and the almost-sex that would have an added frisson, given that it was Paris—and to her shame she wanted it all quite desperately.

But could she really do it? Wouldn't it be the height of selfishness to leave behind her tiny son to go off gallivanting around one of the most romantic cities in the world in search of pleasure, oblivion and her old self?

Well, maybe it would and maybe many would judge her for that, but maybe she ought to give herself a break. Didn't she deserve some fun? And how badly would her absence actually affect Josh? She'd only be away for three days max. Would he even notice? And if he did, would it scar him for life? She didn't think so. She had the utmost faith in Mrs Gardiner, which was ironic when she thought about how suspicious of the whole idea of having a nanny she'd been initially, and there was always the phone. It wasn't exactly difficult to get back from Paris, should for some reason she need to.

'Well?' Finn queried with an arch of an eyebrow that sent thrills of excitement skidding along her veins and a lovely warmth spreading through her body.

'*Oui, d'accord,*' she said, feeling the beginnings of a wide, silly smile spread across her face despite her best efforts to contain it. 'I'd love to.'

At ten o'clock on the following Saturday evening— French time—Georgie was floating on the most incredible high.

She and Finn had arrived in Paris earlier, having caught the train in London and travelled first class. A car had picked them up at the station and had then smoothly whisked them to the latest addition to the Calvert Collection portfolio.

When they'd pulled up outside the Hotel Belle-vue on the Rue du Faubourg Saint-Honoré she'd had trouble keeping her jaw from hitting the floor. The pale, sand-coloured stone of the six-storey building gleamed in the afternoon sun. Each room had a black wrought-iron balcony from which spilled rich red flowers. Some had their red and white striped blinds down, some had their doors open to let in the warm spring breeze. Above the revolving glass and gold front door was a fine black awning, and either side of it stood a tub containing a perfectly clipped ball of a laurel tree. The doorman who tipped his black top hat to them as they approached was wearing a dark coat decorated with gold braid and polished brass. Inside, everything was soft whites and ele-gant *eau-de-nil*, marble floors and sparkling crystal. Beyond the reception desk, through a pair of huge patio doors, Georgie had seen a terrace where tables with bright white parasols had been placed around an area of emerald-green grass bordered with low, neat hedging.

'What do you think?' Finn had asked as they'd gone up in the lift to their suite.

'Breathtakingly stunning.'

'I couldn't agree more,' he'd replied, giving her a direct look that sent heat and desire stealing through her.

The honeymoon suite, which had been put at their disposal, was equally as beautiful with its calming off-white and taupe décor and gorgeous antique furniture. Disappointingly, Finn had disappeared pretty much immediately to go off and do things that, as owner of the hotel, he had to do. But Georgie had managed to occupy herself by exploring the vast suite and terrace, before kicking off her shoes and flopping onto the enormous bed to call Mrs Gardiner for quite possibly the twentieth time.

It hadn't been easy leaving Josh. It had actually been rather more of a wrench than she'd expected. For one dithering moment, just before she'd walked out of the penthouse back in London, she'd genuinely considered going downstairs to where Finn was waiting and telling him to go ahead without her. But Mrs Gardiner had shooed her off, practically locking the door behind her, and so she'd slunk off, torn between wanting to go and guilt at leaving.

That guilt, which had accompanied her throughout the journey to Paris, hadn't fully gone away but she'd been assured during every call she'd subsequently made that her son seemed to be taking their absence in his stride, and finally she'd been able to relax and enjoy the party.

And what a party it was. Five hundred guests, who'd earlier been divided into small groups and given an exclusive tour, now mingled in the ballroom. Members of the waiting staff wove through the journalists, upmarket travel company owners and anyone else lucky enough to have received a coveted invitation, offering up exquisite signature cocktails and the tiniest, most delicious canapés Georgie had ever tasted. She'd laughed and chatted all evening, remembering how much she'd once loved socialising and going giddy with the realisation that it was all coming back to her.

Having Finn at her side helped. His proximity was as reassuring as it was intoxicating. He looked so incredibly handsome this evening in his impeccably tailored navy suit that matched his eyes and a pale blue shirt. His imposing height and the impressive breadth of his shoulders stood him apart from everyone else, and then there was the aura of confidence and power that surrounded him and sent shivers of anticipation rippling through her.

Georgie had only really ever seen Finn the father or Finn the deliverer of outstanding orgasms. She'd never experienced this side of him, the utterly compelling, totally in command, billionaire tycoon. It was dazzling being with him, knowing he was hers, and she was no more immune to his effect than any of the other couple of hundred or so women present this evening.

However, it wasn't the luxury of her surroundings or the endless supply of champagne or even Finn's presence beside her that was causing Georgie's state of heightened excitement. Nor was it the memory of him raising the privacy partition in the car as they'd made their way from the station to the hotel, then sliding his hand up her skirt and making her come silently and hard within minutes, which kept slipping into her head and making her blush. It wasn't even the euphoric relief at knowing she was truly better and could therefore stop taking her medication, a plan she'd implemented this morning.

No.

What was responsible for the dizzying delight whipping through her was the unexpected yet shattering conclusion she'd come to while having her hair and make-up done this afternoon in the hotel's very exclusive salon.

To get there she'd had to pass the hotel's *pharmacie*, which was as elegantly designed as the rest of the building. As she'd settled back to have her hair washed, she'd found herself idly wondering what sort of pharmaceutical things a guest might need while staying in such a hotel but may not have. A forgotten toothbrush perhaps. A plaster or an aspirin. Or something they might possibly need unexpectedly, such as a tampon or, if they were very lucky, a condom. This naturally had got her to thinking about sex, with Finn, how much she longed to do it and what a crying shame it was that they couldn't.

And then it had struck her like a breath-stealing blow to the chest that maybe they could. Her period had finished yesterday—no unexpected need for a tampon—and her cycle was long. So the chances of getting pregnant at this stage of it were remote. Really remote. And therefore if she and Finn were extra-careful, she'd thought, her head spinning and her heart thumping while the stylist lathered her up, what was stopping them from having full-on sex tonight? What was stopping them from making up for lost time and having full-on sex *the entire weekend*?

As far as she could tell, absolutely nothing. It would be virtually risk-free. Certainly risk-free enough for her to consider it an excellent idea. The only potential obstacle was Finn, but surely he wouldn't object. While unravelling her in the car he'd murmured that he'd found the last week impossibly frustrating, despite her extreme and self-less generosity on that front, so presumably he'd be as thrilled with her proposal as she was.

And so, once she was all styled and made up and fairly bubbling over with excitement and anticipation, Georgie had gone back to the pharmacy to acquire supplies for what she hoped would be at least forty-eight hours of mind-blowing sex, give or take a meeting or two, and returned to her room to get dressed as if floating on air.

For the duration of the party she'd hugged her plan to herself, but it wasn't for much longer. In an hour or so the party would surely begin to wind down and they'd be done, and then she and Finn would head upstairs and with any luck start burning up his one thousand thread-count sheets properly.

And, quite frankly, she couldn't wait.

CHAPTER NINE

THERE WAS SOMETHING different about Georgie tonight, Finn thought, watching through narrowed eyes as she chatted and laughed with a small group of guests. And it wasn't just the way she looked, although that was pretty magnificent. The dress she had on was strapless and tight, knee-length and of a forest-green velvety sort of fabric, the kind of dress he wanted to peel off her with his teeth. Nor was it the relaxed ease with which she interacted with people, which reminded him of the vibrant, sexy woman he'd originally met.

Over the last couple of weeks, that Georgie, the one he recognised, had showed increased signs of returning, and he was glad for her sake. And also his, if he was being honest. They might not be having full sex—slightly frustrating although completely understandable—but what they did get up to blew his mind every time. She was so responsive. So enthusiastic. A fascinating and inventive distraction, and just what he'd needed, in fact. Again. Because, what with work and Josh and her, he'd barely had time to think about the progress his investigation agency wasn't making. Nor did he have the head space to continue to mentally rage at Jim and Alice.

The tension that had been gripping him for what felt like decades had begun to lessen and life had become marginally easier in other respects too. While many of the circumstances surrounding his adoption remained painfully confusing, some of the chaos seemed to be settling. He was no longer short with his colleagues and subordinates. He scowled less and his behaviour had become less unpredictable. Only yesterday he'd made a snap decision without even having to think about it, and he was one hundred per cent certain that this was all down to the release he found with Georgie.

Tonight, however, frustratingly, that tension was back. Georgie might look unbelievably beautiful and achingly hot but she kept smiling to herself and drifting off into her own little world, which he found deeply unsettling. He couldn't work out what might have put that sparkle of mischief in her eyes. It couldn't have been the interlude in the car when he hadn't been able to resist touching her. Hours had passed since then. So what was it? He didn't know and he hated it.

But he wouldn't remain in the dark for much longer, he assured himself, his jaw tight. He'd had enough of trying to second guess what Georgie may or may not be planning. All evening he'd been in work mode, ruthlessly focused on the launch, but now the party was coming to an end and he was getting answers.

Taking her elbow and muttering their excuses, he drew her away from the throng and manoeuvred her behind one thick, towering pillar, into the shadows and out of the sight of prying eyes. He backed her up against it, pressed himself close, and she didn't seem to mind.

'What are you up to?' he murmured, planting one hand on the pillar beside her head while wondering where on her body to put the other.

She arched an eyebrow in a way that sent darts of desire shooting through him and smiled up at him coyly. 'What makes you think I'm up to anything?'

'You have a look about you.'

'What kind of a look?'

'As if you're keeping a secret.'

'Maybe I am.'

'I don't like secrets,' he muttered, deciding that high on the curve of her waist with access to the lower side of her breast would be a good place for his hand. He ran his thumb over the soft swell there and the pulse at the base of her neck fluttered.

'You'll like this one,' she said, her voice husky and her eyes darkening.

'What is it?'

'You'll see.' Her gaze dropped to his mouth and he heard her breath catch. 'Are we done here?'

'Nearly.'

'Because I think we should go upstairs. Now.'

'Why?'

'I've recently thought of something else we can try. Something new.'

His pulse thudded heavily and heat infused every inch of him. Something else? Wasn't what they'd already done enough? Was she trying to kill him? 'Like what?' he asked, his body hardening unbearably.

Without taking her eyes off his, she opened her bag, took something out and pressed it into his hand. He glanced down and saw a condom packet in his palm and his heart lurched. 'What's this?'

'Do you really need me to explain?'

Yes, as a matter of fact. 'I thought sex was off the table.'

'It was. But I've reconsidered. I realised this afternoon that it's all about the timing.'

'Which is now?'

She gave a nod. 'It is. And it will be for a couple of days.'

A couple of days? Halle-bloody-lujah. 'Are you sure?'

'Very much so.'

'Then we're going to need a lot more than one.'

'I bought out the pharmacy.'

She was truly unbelievable. 'You know what?' he muttered, practically passing out with the strength of the need now drumming through him. 'I think we're done here.'

To Finn's intense frustration, however, leaving the party took a while. As he strode towards the exit, just about resisting the temptation to drag Georgie along behind him and instead maintaining a civilised although determined speed, people kept coming up to him wanting to chat. Infuriatingly, no one seemed to be deterred either by the electricity he knew was rolling off him or the curtness of his replies. How he managed to refrain from telling everyone to move the hell out of his way so he could get upstairs and ravish the woman at his side he had no idea. The five minutes during which they had to stop and pose for a series of press photographs were quite possibly the longest of his life.

By the time they made it into the lift Finn's jaw was tight and he ached all over with the effort of restraint. Once inside, Georgie took up a position on one mirrored side of the car and he leaned against the opposite wall. Any closer and he might not be able to wait for privacy. He didn't even trust himself to speak, just kept his hand in his pocket, touching the condom, as if not doing so might make it a figment of his imagination. But he didn't take his eyes off her and she didn't stop looking at him, their gazes and their bodies communicating in a way that rendered words unnecessary.

Time passed agonisingly slowly, the space between them filling with tension and vibrating with need, but eventually the lift arrived at their floor. The minute the doors whooshed open, Finn grabbed Georgie's hand and strode towards their room. As soon as he got her inside he had her up against the door and in his arms, their mouths meeting in a hot clash of teeth and tongues that went on and on until his head emptied of everything but her and the clawing need to be inside her.

He ran his hands down her body, moulding them to her shape while she tugged furiously at his shirt. At the feel of her hands on the skin of his back he shuddered and for a moment wanted to pause and revel in her touch, but he wasn't to be distracted. Nothing was going to stop him from ridding of clothes the parts of her he wanted naked.

When he reached her mid-thigh and the fabric of her dress had some give he bunched it in his fists and shoved it up. With a soft, encouraging moan that turned him to granite she edged her legs apart and pushed her hips forwards. He skimmed his hand over the delicate lace of her knickers and she gasped, and when he slipped his fingers beneath the thin waistband her breathing became shallow, her breasts heaving against the restrictive bodice of her dress.

'You're so hot,' he muttered. 'So wet.'

'Stop talking,' she panted.

'No foreplay?'

'Haven't we had enough of that already?'

'More than enough.'

'Then hurry. I'm not sure how much longer I can wait and I *really* want you inside me when I come.'

The desperation he could hear in her voice stoked his desire like a can of petrol being tossed on a bonfire, and the flames raged within him. Shaking slightly, he eased away to yank his trousers and shorts off and roll the condom on while she pushed her knickers down and kicked them to one side. And then he was back in front of her, wrapping his hands around the backs of her thighs and lifting her up.

Their gazes locked as he thrust up and she pushed down, and he saw something hot and unidentifiable flare in the depths of her eyes before she closed them with a soft, ragged groan. Her head thudded against the door as she dropped it back and he couldn't help moving.

Driven on by an urgency and total lack of control he'd never felt before, Finn buried his head in her neck and pulled out of her and then thrust back in, as deep as he could go. He did it again and again, harder and faster, until she was clinging on to his shoulders, her legs tight around his waist, her breath coming in short, sharp pants as she muttered little cries of, 'Oh, God, yes.'

And then suddenly he could feel his orgasm rush towards him with the speed and force of a tsunami and he was too far gone to hold back. Everything inside him tightened, the pressure coiling in his groin so intense that it almost hurt. And when, with a cry, Georgie shattered, trembling in his arms and convulsing around him, he thrust one last time, hard and deep, and erupted as the pleasure hit and spun through him like a starburst.

How long he spent slumped against her in the quiet darkness, his heart thundering in time with hers, he had no idea. After what could well have been the most intense experience of his life, he wasn't capable of thought, much less reason. All he could do was drop his forehead to hers, his breathing harsh and his control in pieces, and whisper, 'You are incredible.'

The following morning when she woke, Georgie stretched and grinned like the cat who'd got the cream, or a woman whose body had been put to thoroughly good use.

Muscles deep inside her ached. She felt all soft and languid and buzzy. Last night had been brilliant. She hadn't realised how frustrating not having full sex had been, but it had clearly been very frustrating indeed, because with the flourishing of that condom she'd unleashed a beast in both of them that had kept going until the early hours of the morning, when they'd both collapsed into a sated, sleepy tangle of sheets. Hard and fast, soft and sensuous, on the bed, in the shower, they'd done it all…

But it wasn't just the mind-blowing sex that had made the night so amazing. It was the realisation she'd just come to that, after months of darkness, there was finally light. Everything was falling into place and, to her giddy relief and delight, the shadows were fading and it felt as if *she* was back.

And, while she didn't know about being incredible, she certainly felt invincible right now, which was in no small part down to the man stretched out beside her, who was sliding a hand down her body and

doing a very good job of making her forget everything but him and her and the way he made her physically feel.

Or, rather, attempting to.

Because she wasn't quite so addled with desire
that she'd forget about her son.

'I should call Mrs G and see how Josh is,' she
murmured, determinedly ignoring the heat beginning to wind through her and reluctantly trying to
ease away from him.

'He'll be fine,' Finn muttered against the sensitive
skin of her neck that he was nuzzling as he clamped
his hands on her hips to hold her still and then rolled
over to pin her to the bed. 'I, on the other hand, am
not,' he said, his eyes dark with need as he looked
down into hers. 'I'm in pain.'

'You're insatiable.'

'That would make two of us, then.'

'A good mother would prioritise her son over sex.'

'You are a good mother.'

'You have to be kidding,' she said, staring up at
him in disbelief. 'I've been a terrible mother.'

'Rubbish.'

'Have you forgotten how Josh and I came into
your life?'

'You were ill.'

'Doesn't matter.'

Clearly realising that sex wasn't happening, although to his credit he didn't emit so much as a whisper of a resigned sigh, Finn lifted himself off her and

lay on his side, propping himself up on his elbow beside her instead.

'Of course it does,' he said, with such certainty that she was almost convinced. 'How's he doing?'

She thought about her happy little boy and the way his tiny, chubby arms lifted up and reached for her when she walked into the room. About how, when she lifted him up, he actually snuggled into her. Josh's well-being couldn't *all* be down to Finn and Mrs Gardiner, could it?

'OK, so maybe I'm not so bad *now*,' she said as a different kind of warmth stole through her, 'but before…'

'Remember your bedsit?'

A picture of peeling paint and threadbare carpet flashed into her head and at the back of her throat she thought she could taste a trace of damp. 'I'd rather not,' she muttered with a shudder, pulling the sheet up to dispel the flurry of goosebumps.

'You weren't going to let me take Josh without you.'

'Well, no, but—'

'Trust me. You're doing fine. And you're around,' he added. 'Which is a plus.'

A shadow flitted across the lean lines of his face and her heart twanged in her chest. 'How did you cope without your mother?'

'I have no idea.'

'But you did.'

'Of course.'

Oh, to have his confidence, she thought wistfully. To not be in doubt about anything or anyone. She'd never met anyone so sure of himself and it was hard not to envy him. 'I was so jealous of you, you know,' she said, shooting him a quick smile.

'When?' he asked with a faint frown.

'Those first few days after we came to stay. When I walked into your kitchen the morning after we arrived and found you feeding Josh so adeptly. There was a time when I couldn't work out which bottle to use or how to mix formula. And then later, being with him, playing with him… You just automatically seemed to know what you were doing and I resented that.'

'Believe me, I didn't.'

'Really?'

'I've never had such a steep learning curve.'

Oh. 'Weirdly, that's good to know. It's easy to assume everyone else has it sorted while you feel like you're floundering, and I floundered more than most for what felt like the longest time.'

'What happened once you got to hospital, Georgie?'

A chill ran through her and she shivered. 'You don't want to know.'

'I do.'

Hmm, that was all very well, but what purpose would it serve either of them? She could see no advantage in rehashing the past. Much of it, blessedly, she couldn't even remember. And, while sharing might have been recommended as therapy, as far as she could see she was doing perfectly well without it. 'Why?'

'I want to know everything about you.'

Oh.

Well.

That was different, then, she thought, her heart slowly turning over as she scoured his eyes, looking for signs of flippancy and finding none. That was shifting this…whatever this was…to another level. And as her heart melted and her resistance evaporated, quite suddenly she wanted to tell him. She wanted him to tell him everything. She didn't want anything to remain between them. He could handle it. He'd handled everything so far with rock-solid strength and complete equanimity, and she rather thought that, even if they hadn't been legally joined, he'd stick it out. She'd trusted him with her body. Surely she could trust him with her secrets.

'It's not pretty,' she warned, nevertheless scarcely able to believe she was going to open the door for him on what had been for her the darkest of times.

'I won't judge.'

'If you did, you'd find me guilty.'

'None of it was your fault.'

'I know that, but that doesn't lessen it.' She swallowed hard to ease the tightness in her throat and took a deep breath. 'I never mentioned how I ended up in hospital in the first place, did I?'

'No.'

'While I was staying with Carla and everything started to fall apart, not only did I begin to behave erratically and have delusions, but I also found myself beginning to really resent Josh. I started to believe that his arrival had ruined everything and...' She paused, momentarily unable to continue, hating herself for what she was about to reveal but reminding herself that it had been a symptom of her illness. 'I didn't want him,' she finished shakily. 'I fantasised about how much easier things would be without him. I became obsessed with leaving him somewhere like outside the hospital and just walking away. One night I even got as far as the bus stop.'

'What happened?'

'Carla showed up and when I told her I was going to the hospital said she'd take me herself. Only when we arrived she had me sectioned.'

'That must have been distressing,' he said, his voice gruff.

'It was. I sort of knew that it was the right thing to be doing but I also hated her for it. The diagnosis that followed was a double-edged sword. On the one hand it was a relief to know there was an explanation for what I was doing and thinking and feeling, but on the other it was a struggle to make sense of it all.' She shook her head and frowned. 'I was supposed to be so *together*. Something like that was never supposed to happen to me. And then it got worse.'

'How?' he asked, his gaze darkening with a concern that heated the chill in her blood and eased the pain of her memories.

'I naively assumed that when it began, the treatment would instantly sort everything out and I'd be better. But it didn't. I was all over the place. For days I'd feel full of energy and be buzzing, convinced that I was doing fantastically. I clearly remember a week or so when my thoughts zipped along, hopping from one to another at incredible speed, and it was so exhilarating to be able to think so fast and so brilliantly. But then I'd suddenly crash to unbelievable lows. I had the most unimaginably horrible hallucinations.'

'About what?'

'Death,' she said. 'My death mainly. I kept having visions of a bunch of doctors and nurses decked out in scrubs and face masks approaching my bed in order to lift me off and put me into the coffin that sat beside it.'

'My God,' he murmured, visibly blanching.

'I did warn you it wasn't pretty,' she said, watching his jaw tighten and his Adam's apple bob as he fought for...well...something. 'The periods in between were filled with the many anxieties I had over Josh. Because of the medication I was on I couldn't breastfeed him. I couldn't interact with him most of the time and I became obsessively worried about how that was going to affect him. Like how he wasn't going to achieve his milestones and things because I wasn't capable of teaching him anything. How badly

I was letting him down. I was also terrified I was going to in some way harm him. Or myself.'

'But that never happened.'

'No.'

'It never would have happened.'

'I have to think not,' she said, determined to believe it. 'Eventually the medication kicked in and suppressed the mania but even that wasn't easy to deal with because it put me in a fog of nothingness which was almost as horrible as what had gone on before. At least then I had the ups.' She fell back against the pillows and gave a sigh of regret and sorrow. 'Looking back, I don't recognise any part of myself. I have no idea who I was. I totally lost me and that makes me sad because I'll never be the person I was before again, and I rather liked her. She was fun and fearless. I'm not even sure who I am now.'

'Josh knows who you are,' he said with quiet conviction.

'That's what the doctors told me. It's taken a while to believe it myself. And to believe that I will be, that I *am*, OK.'

'Are you?'

'I think so,' she said, casting him a small smile. 'But I've been here before. A relapse isn't out of the question. And I worry about getting depression. I've been warned that women who've had post-partum psychosis can end up with bipolar disorder.'

'If any of that happens, I'll be there to catch you. I'll keep you safe.'

He would, wouldn't he? 'Thank you.'

'I should be the one thanking you,' he said gruffly. 'But in all honesty I really don't know what to say.'

'Then why don't you kiss me instead?'

'That I can do.'

He reached out and wrapped a hand around the back of her neck as she moved towards him, and captured her mouth in a soft, soul-stealing kiss that slowly swept away the memories and the anguish and replaced them with a rush of heat and want.

'I'm sorry,' he murmured when they broke for breath.

'What for?'

'Not being there for you.'

'You couldn't have known.'

'The morning after the night we met, just before you left, I was going to suggest we exchange numbers.'

Her eyes widened. 'Were you?'

'I thought about asking you to dinner.'

'Did you? Why?'

'I liked you.'

'It was just sex.'

'No, it wasn't.'

She had to agree, and when she fleetingly thought about what could have been if only she'd had his number her heart squeezed with regret. 'Hindsight is pointless,' she said quietly. 'That me doesn't exist anymore.'

'Yes, she does.'

'She's battered and bruised.'

'She's brave and resilient and stronger than anyone I've ever met.'

God, someone should bottle him. 'I bet you say
that to all the girls.'

'You'd be surprised,' he murmured. 'And in any
case, there hasn't been anyone else since I first met
you a year and a half ago.'

For a moment she just stared at him. 'Are you
serious?'

'Why would I lie?'

A good point. 'Why not?'

'It's been a turbulent time.'

'Your father's illness?'

He hesitated and sympathy tugged at her heart.

'You don't have to talk about it if you don't want
to.'

'I would if I could,' he said, looking utterly, hope-
lessly tortured.

'But you can't so you shan't?'

'Something like that.'

'Too raw?'

He nodded and his eyes filled with bleakness.
'Shattering. In so many ways.'

Overwhelmed with the need to comfort him,
to ease his torment in any way she could, Georgie
shifted and rolled him onto his back, sliding her hand
down the hard planes of his body and watching as
the distress in his expression slowly disappeared.

'What happened to needing to know that Josh is OK?' he said, his voice thick with growing desire.

'We'll definitely call,' she said, giving him a slow smile. 'But later.'

It was quite a bit later when they finally made that call. Shortly afterwards, with great reluctance, Finn dragged himself out of bed and headed off for a meeting with the hotel management, which he had a feeling was going to be a challenge, when all he could think of was Georgie and how she continued to blow his mind.

She might not know who she was, but he did, and he was in awe. He'd never met anyone so insanely tough yet so unbelievably soft. So doggedly determined yet at times so achingly vulnerable. So generous and giving and fearless. Not of the struggles she'd had—those merited every bit of fear she'd felt—but of facing up to them. The way she was able to work through hugely difficult, personal, emotional topics and talk about them was staggering.

How did she *do* that? he wondered as he stepped into the lift and hit the ground floor button. Where did she find the strength to acknowledge her problems and confront them, her shoulders back and head high? He'd never figured out how to achieve any of that. Give him a complex strategic issue and he was all over it. Impossible deals and intransigent planning departments, no problem. A massive upheaval to his personal life, however, with all the tumultuous emotions that came with it, and he fell apart. After everything Georgie had told him about her experiences in hospital, he couldn't even talk about how he felt about Jim's death. He didn't know where to start.

Maybe he ought to ask her for tips. Maybe he ought to open up to her. A little. Because he might as well admit it, he thought, striding through Reception and walking into the meeting room, where a dozen of his staff shot to their feet, it wasn't just sex that had made his life less tense and stressful and somehow better over the last couple of weeks. It was her.

CHAPTER TEN

GEORGIE WHILED AWAY the hours Finn was out mostly by wafting around the suite and reflecting on her Parisian adventure so far, starting with the sex, which had surpassed her wildest expectations, and she'd had a fair few. The night they'd met had been scorching, but now… Well, now, in addition to the red-hot physical chemistry, there was knowing and feeling and, dare she say it, *liking*.

What would have happened if he *had* taken her number that morning? she wondered as she lathered up in the shower and tingled at the memory of Finn's hands on her body. Would they have dated? Would he have somehow noticed what she'd failed to? Could her pregnancy have been as it should have been? It was a pointless exercise if ever there was one, but that didn't stop her imagination playing out the various scenarios or her heart squeezing in response.

Conversely, what if she *hadn't* found him the evening she'd gone looking for him? She liked to think that she'd have muddled through somehow and that she and Josh would have been all right, but life was so much richer, so much brighter for having Finn in it.

Reliving the harrowing details of her stay in hospital had been agonisingly difficult, but ultimately she was glad she'd told him everything. She had no secrets left now and nothing more to hide, and, while she'd taken a massive risk and made herself incredibly vulnerable, she had no doubt that he'd take care of what she'd given him. Not only was he the sexiest man she'd ever met, he was also the most patient and the most understanding.

And then there were the glimpses of his soul that she caught through the tiny cracks that appeared in his armour from time to time. Beneath his brusque and aloof exterior lay a seething mass of emotion, she was sure. The issues he clearly had surrounding the death of his father made her heart wrench every time she recalled how desolate and devastated he'd looked, lying there next to her.

He was everything she could possibly ask for in a co-parent or a lover yet the things she found most attractive about him had nothing to do with Josh or his devastating looks and wicked bedroom skills and everything about who he fundamentally was. He took his responsibilities seriously. His support was steadfast. She had no doubt she would always be able to depend on him.

Little wonder, then, that she was beginning to fall for him.

And, as if all that wasn't enough to make her heart melt like butter over heat, Finn was now feeding her. When he'd returned from his meeting he'd announced that he was taking her out to lunch and told her to hop to it.

It was a glorious spring day so they'd walked, taking in the gardens and the parks and lingering in the Jardin des Tuileries, before being seated on the terrace of the fanciest restaurant she'd ever been to. While a string quartet nearby played something light and uplifting Finn tucked into a plate of seabass and she tried not to devour her delicious seared tuna too greedily.

The weekend was turning out to be as wonderful and romantic as Georgie had imagined, maybe even more so, and she was so overwhelmed by it that she thought she'd best stick to business before she did something unwise like tell him how she was beginning to feel about him.

'So, was the launch considered to be a success?' she asked, putting her fork down on her empty plate and taking a sip of crisp chilled Chablis in an effort to appear cool and collected.

'Yes.'

'Is anything you do *not* a success?'

He flashed her a quick smile that set off fireworks in the pit of her stomach. 'Rarely.'

'And again, I envy you,' she said with a sigh.

'Why?'

'It feels like a long time since anything I did was successful.'

'Not from where I'm sitting,' he said, giving a nod of thanks to the waiter who cleared their table, then sitting back and eyeing her thoughtfully. 'You know, we're very similar, you and I.'

She felt her eyebrows shoot up. Seriously? Finn was a put-together billionaire who knew exactly who he was and where he was going. She was still a bit of a mess who knew next to nothing about anything. She could see no similarity whatsoever. 'Are we?' she said sceptically. 'How?'

'We're both survivors.'

'I suppose,' she said, although she still didn't really know enough about him to judge.

'But that's not all. We're both determined. Both ambitious. We've both come a long way and done it with little outside support.'

Hmm. 'Well, I might have been all that once upon a time,' she conceded, wondering whether that might be why she felt such a strong sense of recognition whenever she looked at him. 'But I'm not sure about now.'

'You will be again.'

'Not in the field of law,' she said, nevertheless warmed by his belief in her. 'My career in that is pretty much over, I suspect. I was sectioned. I haven't looked into it but it wouldn't surprise me if that didn't disqualify me from practising. And I doubt I'd get a glowing reference from my last company anyway.'

'Want me to take them on?'

'Why not?' she said with a grin.

'I mean it.'

Her grin faltered and her heart gave a great thump. 'Would you do that?'

'All you have to do is say the word and they're history.'

As if she needed a reminder of his power and influence or another reason to fall a little bit more in love with him. 'Thank you, but no.'

'Sure?'

'Yes.'

'Shame.'

'I'll figure something out workwise,' she said, forcing herself to focus on something other than how giddy she felt at having someone on her side for possibly the first time in her life, at being part of a team. 'Maybe I'll retrain and do something to help people who are going through what I did. I had amazing care. I'd like to give something back. Maybe I could fundraise or something.'

'Let me know what I can do to help.'

He already had, more than he could possibly know. 'I will,' she said with a smile.

His gaze dropped to her mouth then, his eyes darkening in a way that never failed to render her hot and breathless. 'Let's have dessert back at the hotel,' he said, and called for the bill.

Quite some time later, as Georgie lay sprawled across the bed, unable to move for lazy lethargy, it occurred to her that the thing that had been bubbling away inside her all day, filling her with light and hope, was happiness. She was happy. Actually happy. Her confidence and self-esteem were soaring and it felt as though her demons were finally in retreat, which only went to show how very good for her Finn was.

She'd had the best day, and now, as she listened to the sound of the shower and contemplated joining him in it, she couldn't help wondering if there was anything stopping them from turning this relationship that had started for the benefit of Josh into one that also benefited them. Because not only was she happy, but Finn too seemed remarkably content with the way things were. He was certainly less stressed and more relaxed than he'd been a month or so ago.

They appeared to be on the same wavelength and there was lust and there was trust and possibly even the beginnings of love, so who knew? Their relationship could go anywhere, and she cautiously examined the heart-thumping idea that the tight, stable, supportive family unit she'd always longed for might actually be within her grasp for the first time in her life.

Closing her eyes, she tried envisaging it, and it wasn't that hard because her common sense was no match for the allure of that which she craved deep inside. Within minutes she had herself and Finn and Josh living in a gorgeous house in the country filled with laughter and lust and love in a place where it was perpetual summer and the birds didn't stop singing.

It was a heady, if utterly unreal, bubble and one

that kept expanding preposterously until it abruptly burst when Finn's phone started buzzing its way across the bedside table. The phone fell to the floor before she could reach it, but she leaned down to pick it up anyway, and as she did so, out of the corner of her eye, she caught sight of the caller.

Osborne Investigations.

The name sparked something in the dusty recesses of her memory.

What was it?

Hmm...

Oh, yes.

The night he'd scooped her and Josh up and whisked them to his hotel. The night she'd been left with no option but to tell him where she'd been and what she'd been doing because if she hadn't he'd have had an investigating agency on to it so fast it would make her head spin.

That was it.

But what could Finn possibly need investigating? she wondered, replacing his phone on the bedside table and lying back against the pillows. Was it something to do with work? A person? A company? Or something else entirely? It was none of her business, of course, yet she couldn't help but be curious. She was curious about everything to do with him.

'Why do you have an investigation agency working for you?' she asked when he emerged from the bathroom in a cloud of steam and a fluffy white towel wrapped around his hips, a sight she didn't think she'd ever tire of.

He visibly tensed, and all the little hairs at the back of her neck stood up in response to the conclusion that she was on to something interesting. 'Why do you ask?'

'Your phone vibrated and then fell on the floor, so I picked it up. Their name was on the screen.'

He went even stiller and seemed to pale. 'Did you answer it?'

'Of course not.'

'When did they ring?'

'About a minute ago.'

'Right.' He tossed the towel onto the bed and, to her disappointment, since it clearly meant that some more of that lovely, headboard-banging sex was temporarily off the agenda, spun away to don a pair of jeans and a shirt.

'Well?' she prompted.

'Excuse me,' he muttered distractedly as he strode to the bedside table and grabbed his phone. 'I need to return that call.'

With the last twenty-four hot, intense and strangely perturbing hours instantly wiped from his mind, Finn stalked out of the bedroom, across the hall, and into the sitting room. He closed the door behind him with deliberate control, his gut churning and his pulse racing. Alexandra Osborne called him once a week, same time, same day, regardless of whether

she'd made progress, and Sunday evening at six—
or five p.m. back home—was neither that day nor
that time.

Beginning to pace up and down, he located the
missed call and returned it, and when she answered
said, 'What do you have for me?'

'You might want to sit down,' she replied without preamble.

He drew to an abrupt halt and dropped into the
nearest available chair. 'Go ahead.'

'Early last week one of the leads we've been working on finally came good.'

'In what way?'

'It's been established that your adoptive parents
visited Argentina six months after you were born.
They went on their own and returned with you.'

The world skidded to a standstill and his heart
gave a great lurch. Argentina? What the hell?

'My contact managed to trace their movements
while they were there,' Alex continued while Finn
grappled for calm and forced himself to focus, 'and
placed them in La Posada.'

'Which is what?'

'A small, abandoned village near the border with
Bolivia. It consists mainly of a derelict orphanage
and a handful of ruined houses. While most of it was
looted years ago, the office of the orphanage had
barely been touched, quite probably because the filing cabinets had been bolted to the walls. In amongst

the papers they contained he found a number of birth certificates. We believe one of them to be yours.'

His lungs tightened. A punch of adrenaline kicked him in the chest and his pulse raced. 'How can you be sure?'

'The recorded date of birth is a match.'

'Does it have the names of the parents?'

'Yes. Juan Rodriguez and Maria Gonzalez. I'll email you a copy of everything we have. I apologise for it taking so long. The trail has been extremely well buried. We're still working on why that would be the case.' Alex paused, while Finn reeled, then said, 'There's something else.'

'What?'

'Are you still sitting down?'

'Yes.'

'There were two other birth certificates in the same file. Both boys. All of you born at around the same time on the same day.'

It took a second or two for the implication of what she was saying to sink in, but when it did the ground beneath his feet tilted violently. His vision blurred and he could hardly breathe. He felt as if he was about to pass out. 'I have brothers?'

'It would appear so. The evidence would suggest you're triplets.'

'Where are they? Are they alive?'

'Impossible to know at this stage.'

'Find them,' he said, his voice thick and his throat

clogging. 'Whatever you have to do, however much you have to pay, find them.'

'We will.'

Finn ended the call and as the phone slipped out of his hand and fell to the floor, the calm front he'd presented to Alex shattered. Every bit of him started shaking. His heart was beating too fast. His stomach was roiling. He was going to throw up.

Blindly, he got to his feet and made it to the terrace doors, which he threw open, and gulped in some much needed air while the information he'd just been given went round and round in his thoughts.

He'd been born in South America. He'd spent time in an orphanage. He had parents, brothers, was one of a set of triplets. Identical? Non-identical? What had happened to the other two? Where were they and why had they been separated?

The ping of an incoming message on his phone pierced the fog swirling around in his head and he stumbled back to where he'd been sitting. With trembling fingers he bent down to pick the device up and then collapsed into the chair before his legs gave way. Somehow he managed to unlock it. Somehow he found the right app, tapped the email and, his heart thundering so fast and hard it hurt, opened the attachment.

It contained three birth certificates plus translations. All identical, save the times of birth and the names. Mateo. Diego. Juan. His parents, his brothers, his family.

But which was his? Who was he and where were the others? Above all, *why*? Why the adoption? Why the separation? And who'd known? Had Jim and Alice been aware he was one of three? Surely not. Surely they couldn't have been so cruel as to keep that from him. Yet no one had ever mentioned Argentina. He even had a hotel there. In Buenos Aires. Jim had been at the opening six years ago and he'd never said a thing.

Having scoured the details and committed them to memory, Finn dropped the phone again, then rubbed his hands across his face and leaned forwards, his elbows resting on his knees, his head buried in his hands. How the hell was he going to deal with this? He'd assumed that with information would come clarity, but he was wrong. That assumption had been based on the most simple of explanations, yet the news Alex had just delivered threw up an explanation that was anything but simple.

Instead of being answered and filed away for cool, calm analysis, the questions were multiplying, ricocheting around his head faster and more chaotically and he couldn't sort any of them out. It was all too huge, too overwhelming.

As was the pain now beginning to slice through him as the shock-induced numbness faded. Thirty-one years he'd lost. Thirty-one years that he could potentially have known his siblings, his brothers. He could have had an entire other life. Would it have been better? Worse? It didn't matter. He'd been denied the choice because of Jim and Alice's silence, and the sense of betrayal that he assumed had abated now flayed him all over again, ripping open old wounds and stabbing at them afresh.

He'd thought he had it all under control, but he didn't. He had nothing under control. The pain powering through him was like a living thing, writhing around in his belly and thundering along his veins, leaving every inch of him raw and exposed and bleeding.

'Are you all right?'

At the sound of Georgie's voice, filled with concern, coming from far, far away, Finn froze. He hadn't heard the door open. He hadn't noticed the shadows lengthening across the floor. She couldn't see him like this, he thought frantically, a cold sweat breaking out all over his skin—weak, vulnerable and suffering, a man on the brink of collapse. He couldn't let her help. He couldn't allow her to push and prod as she was wont to do. It would drive him over the edge.

'Get out,' he said, his voice hoarse and cracked.

'What's happened?' she said, walking into the room and dropping to her knees beside the chair in which he was sitting, crowding his space and his thoughts, too close, too dangerous.

'I said, get out.'

'I know. But you're white as a sheet and shaking. I'm worried about you.'

'I'm fine.'

'Talk to me.'

'It has nothing to do with you,' he said sharply, desperately, seeing her flinch, which only added to his torment.

'Try.'

His strength was failing. His control was unravelling. He didn't have much time. 'No.'

'Yes.'

'All right,' he said harshly, his resistance crumbling beneath the need to get her out of his space before he completely lost it. 'How's this? Last November I discovered that I was adopted at the age of six months and that my entire life has been a lie. Fifteen minutes ago I learned that not only was I born in Argentina and left in an orphanage, but that I also have two brothers. We're triplets. As you may be able to understand, it's quite a lot to take in. I need some time and space to process it. So I'd appreciate it if you would respect that and leave me the hell alone.'

Wow.

Just wow.

For the briefest of moments all Georgie could do was stare at Finn as the frustration and torment rolled off him in waves and engulfed her, the shock of what he'd told her and how brutally he'd delivered it rendering her immobile. She could barely process it. He'd been adopted? He'd just found out he had a family he'd known nothing about? No wonder he was in such a spin.

When she'd seen the man she was in love with hunched over like that, clearly hurting, clearly in pain, her heart had twisted, and even though she hadn't known what was troubling him, she'd just felt a clamouring urge to race over and give him a hug. All she wanted to do was help. Genuinely.

But he didn't want it, she realised, the breath catching in her throat as her chest tightened. He didn't want comfort. He didn't want anything from her, as was clear not only from his words but also from the way he was jerking to his feet, turning away from her and stalking over to the window, a blunt, brutal dismissal that sliced her in two.

To think she'd been worried about him, she thought, her eyes stinging and hurt scything through her as she pushed herself to her feet and took a shaky step back. That all the time she'd spent showering and dressing while the minutes ticked slowly by she'd been wondering whether he was all right. What a waste of time and effort that had been.

He didn't want her and he certainly didn't need her. He probably never had. He was wholly self-contained. And as for the idea that they might be embarking on something resembling a proper relationship, what had she been *thinking*?

There may be lust but there was certainly no trust. Not on his side anyway. He must have been carrying the burden of his adoption for months, and the discovery of it, the uncertainty surrounding his identity, must have been cataclysmic. And he hadn't said a word. She'd told him virtually everything there was to know about her, warts and all, and he'd revealed practically nothing.

Every time he'd asked her something about herself she'd spouted like a fountain. She'd told him things, this morning in particular, that she'd never told anyone, things that she'd only just begun to acknowledge. Yet when the tables were turned and she dared to ask him anything even *remotely* personal he deflected it. She knew next to nothing about his upbringing or his parents or how he felt about any of it. How had she let that happen?

And why had he never told her that he was adopted? He'd told her that he didn't like secrets, but he'd been harbouring a massive one of his own, and on top of everything else that made him a hypocrite. So who else knew? Was she the only one who didn't? Why hadn't he wanted to talk about it with her? What was wrong with her? Was it the state of her mental health? Was that why he'd told her he wanted to know everything about her when they'd been talking this morning? She'd seen his interest as a sign their relationship was shifting to another, more intimate level but perhaps he'd just been looking out for Josh by trying to find out how stable she really was?

They had no relationship and no connection, she realised as she stalked into the bedroom, blinking rapidly to ease the prickling in her eyes, and she'd been a fool to even begin to think otherwise. Everything she'd stupidly imagined they'd shared was entirely one-sided. Even this weekend, which had meant so much to her, would now be nothing more than a permanently tarnished memory.

She'd been falling for an illusion, a man who didn't exist, a man she'd conjured up out of her own imagination because that was what she needed. She'd been delusional, which wasn't a word she used lightly, and worse, naive. What would someone like Finn with his gorgeous looks and confidence and billions in the bank ever see in a woman like her anyway? How could her judgement still be so off?

Well, no more, she thought grimly, grabbing her suitcase and depositing it on the bed. Enough of the imbalance. Enough of being the pathetic, soppy drip she turned into around him. If she didn't want to end up being even more hurt, perhaps even irreparably so, she could afford neither.

Nor was she having her recently rediscovered confidence and self-esteem knocked by Finn and his stick-his-head-in-the-sand attitude. She had to protect herself, although how she was going to do that now that they were civilly partnered and therefore stuck with each other and living in close proximity she had no idea. But she'd think of something. She'd have to.

In the meantime there was no way she was hang-

LUCY KING 179

ing around like a punchbag for all the emotions he must be feeling and clearly couldn't handle. She was packing up and going back to London. Back to her son, who, unlike Finn, *did* need her. And then Finn would have all the space and time to think that he wanted.

CHAPTER ELEVEN

FINN STOOD AT the window and stared blankly onto the streets of Paris stretching out far below, the silence telling him that Georgie had finally done what he'd needed her to do and in the nick of time. Treachery, hurt and sadness had wound their tendrils along every vein and around every cell, and he felt shattered, broken, as though he was being pummelled to within an inch of his life.

He had to calm down, he told himself desperately, forcing himself to take a deep, shuddering breath and loosen his white-knuckled fists. He had to stop. For the sake of his blood pressure and the woman he'd sent away, who was no doubt cursing him with every breath she took. He couldn't go on like this, snapping and snarling in a way he thought he'd long since buried. He'd hated that man. He wouldn't allow himself to regress again.

As he battled to control the pandemonium churning him up inside, he thought too how he hated the way he'd responded to Georgie's offer of help. How savagely he'd lashed out at her. At the memory of the way in which he'd spoken to her, he inwardly cringed. She'd done nothing to deserve such treatment. All she'd wanted was to help.

And maybe, despite his assertions to the contrary, he needed it. Because he didn't hold much hope of sorting the turmoil out on his own. He didn't exactly have a great track record on that front. He'd bottled up how he'd felt about his mother's death. He'd pushed aside his father's diagnosis initially with alcohol and sex and, subsequently, work. He'd responded to the discovery of his adoption by being unpleasantly short and rude to anyone who had the misfortune of finding themselves in his vicinity.

What he hadn't done was talk about it. Any of it. To anyone. He didn't do talking. He never had done. His father had been the stoical, stiff-upper-lip type, unable to show emotion. Even when Finn's mother had died, he'd hidden his grief behind a wall of impenetrability. As a result, when it came to feelings, Finn had always been self-reliant, a master of internalisation, choosing to box up what he felt so as not to have to deal with the inevitable messy fallout.

Only this morning—God, was it only this morning?—he'd considered perhaps asking Georgie for tips, and if ever there was an occasion to do so, this was it. Who better to talk to? She knew what it was like to stumble around blindly, looking for answers. She knew him. And, more to the point, for some unfathomable reason he *wanted* her to know. They were a team. In this thing, whatever it was, together.

He was under no illusion that it would be easy. It would probably be hell on earth, even assuming that Georgie was receptive to the idea, which was doubtful, given how he'd dismissed her. But it was worth a shot. He had to do *something* that made sense. And at the very least he owed her an apology.

Finally finding a path through the chaos, Finn spun round and strode out of the sitting room and into the bedroom, only to come to an abrupt halt at the sight of Georgie packing a suitcase.

'What are you doing?' he said, his brows snapping together in a deep frown.

She didn't look at him, just carried on folding the stunning green dress she'd worn last night and which he'd peeled off her what felt like a lifetime ago.

'What does it look like?' she said, her voice utterly devoid of the warmth and concern with which she'd asked him what was wrong back there in the sitting room.

'You're packing.'

'Yes.'

'Why?'

'You wanted space. You wanted time. I plan to give you both.'

What? 'I meant I needed a couple of minutes,' he said. 'Ten. Maybe fifteen. I didn't mean for you to leave.'

'Well, there seems little point in hanging around.'

At the realisation that she actually meant it he felt a sharp stab of something to the chest, and for a moment he thought, well, of course she was. Leaving was what people who he cared about or who were supposed to care about him did, after all. But he shoved it aside in order to focus because this was one occasion at least in which he *did* have the power to take control. 'Don't go.'

'Give me one good reason not to.'

'You were right. I think I probably should talk to someone.'

She flung her hairbrush into the case, then whirled round to scoop up her make-up that was scattered on the dressing table. 'So find a therapist,' she said, dumping it in there too.

'But you're here.'

'Right.'

'Please. I'm sorry for lashing out,' he said, his jaw clenching as he recalled how he'd spoken to her. 'I didn't handle things well.'

'It's fine.'

'It isn't.'

She shrugged. 'You'd had a shock.'

That was an understatement. 'Nevertheless, it's no excuse,' he said gruffly. 'I really am sorry.'

'Apology accepted. Now, if you wouldn't mind…'

'Please, Georgie.'

She must have heard the note of torment in his voice because she stopped what she was doing, *finally*, and gave a great sigh. 'OK, fine,' she said, abruptly sitting on the bed and looking at him, her eyes wary and her expression cool. 'God knows you've had to listen to me prattle on enough.' *Prattle?* he thought with a frown. She did *not* prattle. 'So if you want to talk I'll listen.'

With a rush of relief, Finn stalked into the room and leaned against the edge of the dressing table she'd just cleared. He rubbed his hands over his face and then shoved them into the pockets of his jeans. He cleared his throat and braced himself.

'So it turns out that I find it hard to process big things,' he began, inwardly wincing at how pathetic he sounded. 'Especially big *emotional* things. I have a tendency to lock things down.'

'That's understandable. Although probably not very healthy.'

'No.' It wasn't healthy at all. God only knew the damage he'd caused his nervous system recently. It also smacked of hypocrisy because it had just occurred to him that by withholding the truth from her and obfuscating he'd been behaving like Jim and Alice, which did not sit well.

'Have you always done it?'

He gave a short nod. 'Ever since my mother—Alice—died.'

'That's a long time.'

'Yes.' Too long, with hindsight. 'I bottled up how I felt about that for years. I was only ten. I didn't know what the hell was going on. Jim—my father—

or, rather, my adopted father—did the best he could but he wasn't one for emoting either.'

Her eyebrows lifted. 'You didn't talk to anyone? A counsellor? A teacher?'

He shook his head. 'No one. Not until the lid of the pressure cooker flew off when I was a teenager.'

'What happened then?'

'Nothing all that dramatic. I got into a couple of fights when I was sixteen. Spent a night in jail for being drunk and disorderly.'

'And then you had therapy?'

'Of a kind. The officer in charge that night asked what I was thought I was doing and it all came out. She gave me some good advice. The incident turned out to be a huge wake-up call. However, it turns out that internalising things is a hard habit to break.'

'We all have our ways of coping.'

Yes, well, unlike hers, his weren't working out so well. 'Jim's diagnosis was something else I didn't talk about,' he said, forcing himself to keep going because she needed to know everything in order to be able to help.

'Did no one ask?'

'Not many knew. I told the people who did that everything was fine.'

'So how did you find out you were adopted?'

'I was going through Jim's papers after he died. The certificate was in a box that had been stored in the attic of his house.'

'That must have been devastating.'

'It was. I was in the middle of a full-blown identity crisis when you turned up with the news about Josh.'

'No wonder you were so insistent on rescuing him. He's your only flesh and blood.'

'As far as I know.'

She frowned and gave a faint nod. 'Right.'

Unable to bear the intensity of her scrutiny or suppress the restlessness whipping around inside him any longer, Finn pushed himself off the dressing table. 'It's been a disorientating time,' he said, shoving his hands through his hair as he began to pace. 'I feel as if I've been manipulated. As though everything about me has to be redefined and renegotiated. I'm thirty-one. It's been tough trying to work out how much of my life has been real and how much a lie. I can't figure out why Jim never said anything, especially after Alice died, and it's been driving me mad.'

Georgie gave a loud sigh of what sounded like exasperation. 'Oh, for the love of God, will you *please* stop calling them that?' she said heatedly.

Stunned at her tone, wondering where the hell the sympathy he'd been expecting was, Finn came to an abrupt halt and whipped round to stare at her. 'What?'

Her colour was high and her eyes were blazing and the need that suddenly streaked through him nearly knocked him off his feet. 'Look, Finn, I get that you feel let down and betrayed. And, believe me, I know what it's like to have your whole world turned upside down and your identity stripped away. But Jim and Alice were, to all intents and purposes, your parents.'

He ruthlessly quashed the desire and frowned at her, denial reeling through him. 'I fail to see how.'

'Biology doesn't automatically grant parental rights,' she said bluntly. 'Nor does it guarantee the ability to parent successfully. Look at mine. They're hardly an advert for parents of the year. They never gave a toss about me, not properly, and they still don't. Carla's looked out for me far more than they ever did. She's the reason I was able to find you all those weeks ago. If she hadn't made me send her a photo of you along with your name the night we met, things could have turned out very differently. You had two people who loved and cared for you. And, yes, then, tragically, only one, but nevertheless you had someone on your side for *years*, someone who by your own admission never failed to support and champion you when it mattered most. You honestly don't know how lucky you were.'

'What if my mother's death wasn't an accident?' The question shot out of his mouth before he could stop it and he froze, every muscle in his body as taut as a bow string.

'What do you mean?' she asked carefully and he suddenly found himself on a knife edge.

He could easily deflect the question, he knew, but what would be the point of that? He needed her perspective and her insight into things he couldn't make head or tail of, and that meant unlocking the doors on his greatest concerns and flinging them open, so he took a deep breath and said, 'What if she killed herself deliberately because of me, because of what I was or wasn't?'

He hated the catch he could hear in his voice, but he didn't regret the question because her face softened and, ah, there was the sympathy he'd been in need of. 'Do you really believe that?'

'I don't know.'

'What do you remember of her?'

He scrolled back twenty years, searching for memories that were faded and hazy but nevertheless still there. 'She smelled of roses,' he said eventually. 'She taught me poker and played football with me. Every Saturday she'd bake brownies.'

'She sounds lovely,' Georgie said, a trace of wistfulness flitting across her face.

'She was.'

'Did she make you eat your vegetables?'

'Yes.'

'Make you do your homework and go to bed on time?'

'Yes.'

'Were you ever sent to your room or grounded?'

'Frequently.'

'Then she loved you,' she said with quiet conviction. 'Very much. Take it from someone who knows what it feels like not to matter. They must have wanted you very much too, to go all the way to Argentina to fetch you. And they must have had their reasons for keeping it from you.'

'I guess I'll never know,' he said, his throat oddly tight.

'Unless your investigation agency digs something up.'

'Maybe not even then.'

'So much in life we just have to accept.'

'As I'm discovering.'

'Me too.'

With a strangely sad sort of smile she pushed herself off the bed and returned her attention to the suitcase, and as he watched her pull the top down and zip it up it hit him like a blow to the chest that, despite everything he'd just revealed, nothing had changed.

'You're still planning to leave?' he asked, the blade of rejection slicing through him like a knife.

'I have to get back to Josh.' She shot him a quick glance, full of something he was too stung, too busy reeling, to identify. 'Unless there's any other reason for me to stay?'

'No, nothing,' he said, coolly, calling himself a fool for wanting her to stay, for thinking that he was good enough for her, for believing that they were in this together. 'Go. Please. Don't let me stop you.'

All she'd wanted was for him to say that he wanted her to stay, thought Georgie numbly as she stepped off the train at St Pancras and, dragging her wheelie case behind her, went in search of a taxi. That they were a team. A tightly knit unit. That she mattered to him as much as he mattered to her, despite her best efforts to deny it.

But he'd let her go with such ease, and that hurt unbelievably badly. So much for thinking that she could somehow avoid more pain, that she could protect herself. Or that she was only beginning to fall for him. She already had. There could be little doubt about it. She had to be head over heels in love with him for his indifferent dismissal to cause this much agony.

But however much it hurt, the pain wouldn't last because that love hadn't been real. Finn wasn't the man she'd thought him to be. She'd given him attributes—loyalty, honesty, integrity—that he didn't have, and really she had no one to blame but herself. She was the one who'd placed him on a pedestal so high and wobbly that it was inevitable he should fall off it. She was the one who'd misread every look and every word, reading things into his actions that simply hadn't been there. This whole mess was entirely her fault.

The train journey from Paris had lasted two and a half hours and every minute of it she'd spent analysing their relationship, such as it was. And she could see now that she'd been a fool. Finn had never wanted her. Not really. All he wanted was Josh. She came as part of the package and was handy for sex, but that was about it.

She knew this to be true because right from the start she'd been the one in the driving seat. In the bar the night they'd first met she'd been the one to approach him, and then the one to proposition him by telling him she wanted to leave, with him. He hadn't chosen her that night. She'd chosen him.

And so it had been ever since.

She'd given him no option but to take up the role of father and provide his support. What else could he have done in the circumstances? How could she have forgotten the reluctance with which he'd taken her in along with Josh? How she'd made him spend his evenings with her and then virtually forced him into going to bed with her by following him into his room the night he'd told her to put on a dressing gown and whipping her top off? Ditto when she'd pressed the condom into his hand at the party last night and told him she wanted sex. He hadn't even planned to take her to Paris. The invitation had been last-minute and he'd only asked her because of what they'd been getting up to after dark.

And then take this evening, when he'd finally opened up to her about how he felt about his parents and the revelations surrounding his adoption. He'd only done that because she was there. Because she was convenient. He hadn't particularly wanted to talk to *her*.

He'd volunteered nothing willingly, she could see now. He obviously didn't see her as an equal in this relationship. Maybe not in anything. They weren't partners in any sense of the word. They were nothing. She was nothing. And so, frankly, what was the point in them continuing with this ridiculous charade?

CHAPTER TWELVE

FINN SPENT THE torturous hours following Georgie's departure railing at himself while ploughing through half a bottle of Scotch. He'd been a fool for telling her everything. He'd made himself insanely vulnerable and unacceptably weak. He'd invested too much in the power of her response, and, unlike any other he'd ever made, that investment had badly backfired. The hurt and disappointment that roared through him when he recalled how carelessly she'd left him were precisely why he didn't share. How could he have forgotten that? At what point had he recklessly decided to ignore what he knew to be true—that other people's behaviour was incalculable and that the only person he could rely on was himself? What had he been thinking?

All in all, he was glad she'd gone. He had a hectic schedule over the next couple of days and he needed to focus. He did not need extra stress and he did not need Georgie. He was perfectly capable of working through everything going on in his head on his own. It might take some time, but he was going to let it play out and eventually he'd get there. He had to obliterate the ridiculous feelings of rejection and abandonment, and regroup.

However, with increasing frequency, he found himself revisiting their conversation, assessing what Georgie had said and stripping the words of emotion. Grudgingly, he came to the conclusion that she'd had a point. Possibly even more than one. Because the truth was that, however hard he looked, however much money he threw at the investigation, he may never get the answers he sought.

So what was he going to do? He couldn't spend the rest of his life being bitter and resentful. He had to accept that he'd become the man he was now because of Jim and Alice, who *had* been his parents in all ways that counted. The memories he had of his mother were warm and happy. The photos they'd taken of him had filled dozens of albums. His father had not once let him down while alive. He'd been an unfailing tower of strength. Only in death had he turned out to have feet of clay. But as neither of them was around to defend or explain their actions and decisions, what had gone before was beyond Finn's control.

How he went forward, however, *was* within his control. Whatever the reasons for his adoption and the subsequent secrecy surrounding it, he had to forgive his parents, his father in particular. He could understand now a paternal determination to protect a child to the exclusion of all else. To not let anything upset the status quo. Whatever else he might think, he had to understand that none of it was anything to do with him and believe it. His parents had done their best and they'd been good people, and Georgie was right: he had been lucky. It was all right to regret that his father had never got to meet Josh and it was all right to resume the grieving process that had been interrupted with the discovery of that certificate.

He had to let it go and focus on the family he did have instead of chasing relentlessly after wisps of the one he may or may not have elsewhere. He had so much to appreciate. So much to value.

Especially Georgie.

Who, despite her apparent rejection, despite his attempts to put her out of his mind, he was missing more than he could have ever imagined. He'd got used to having her around, in his home and in his bed, and he felt her absence like a physical loss. It was more than just the phenomenal sex he missed. He missed her wit and her smile, her wisdom, the way she challenged him and made him face up to things he'd rather ignore, and the conversations that had relaxed and deepened with time. Their relationship might have started out as one of convenience for the sake of Josh but it wasn't any longer. They knew every inch of each other's bodies. And minds. He'd trusted her with his secrets and she'd trusted him with hers, her honesty so raw that it had torn at his soul and filled him with even more burning regret that his support had come so late.

Finn had never been in love before. He'd never even so much as thought about it, so he had nothing with which to compare the feelings that were swirling around inside him, feelings that were so intense, so powerful they couldn't be locked away even if he tried. Nevertheless he was now pretty sure that the way his heart leapt whenever she walked into the room, the unrelenting need, the respect and admiration he had for her, and the hammering desire to protect her and grow old with her met the definition of it. So too did the happiness and sense of rightness that spread through him whenever she entered his head, which was virtually all the time. And when he thought about the shimmering warmth with which he occasionally caught her looking at him and the way her eyes sparkled when she was with him he was equally sure that she felt the same way about him.

Or at least she had done.

Until he'd behaved like an idiot and let her go. Even if he hadn't realised at the time quite why he needed her, he should have come up with a reason for her to stay. As she'd asked. A request, which, now he thought about it, now he could clearly recall how she'd put it, had been made with the answer she wanted in mind. Of course, it was entirely possible that she *had* simply wanted to get back to Josh. But equally, what if she'd wanted something else entirely? What if he'd allowed his insecurities to dominate and had overreacted? What if she hadn't been rejecting *him*, but the abominable way he'd behaved? More importantly, what might have happened if he hadn't let her go?

As Finn strode out of the hotel on Tuesday afternoon and climbed into the car he thought with grim determination that there was only one way to find out whether or not he'd ruined things with Georgie for good. And, since he was now through with boxing up emotion and ignoring it, however difficult, he was going to take it.

Finn had texted her earlier to say that he was on his way home and had given her an ETA, but Georgie, who was sitting cross-legged on the sofa and staring into space, couldn't summon up the energy to care. The last couple of days hadn't been easy. In fact, apart from the time she spent with Josh, they'd been miserable. She felt so cold, so tired. What with all the thinking she'd been doing about her and Finn, she hadn't been sleeping too well, and watching out for Josh, who'd started crawling and was constantly getting to places he shouldn't, was exhausting. This morning she'd barely managed to haul herself out of bed when her son had called for her for the fifth time in as many hours.

Contrary to her expectations, the disappointment and sadness she felt at knowing that the man she'd fallen in love with didn't exist hadn't faded. Everything had worsened and then amalgamated and now thrashed around in the pit of her stomach, giving her no respite. The delirious happiness she'd once thought she felt had been nothing but an illusion. The realisation that the secure, loving family unit she craved was as distant a possibility as it ever had been was devastating.

Nothing she did alleviated the gloom. She'd tried writing about how she felt in her journal but the last two days' pages were blank. She didn't know where to begin. Going out and getting some fresh air seemed like a huge effort, so she hadn't bothered. Even venturing onto the terrace presented a mammoth challenge. She certainly hadn't had the energy to pack up with Josh and leave, as she'd originally planned. And in any case, where would she have gone? She could hardly move into a different hotel room, and Carla would ask too many questions that Georgie wouldn't be able to answer. Besides, she and Finn needed to unpick this disaster of an arrangement and sooner rather than later.

She fed Josh and changed him and played with him, but she felt oddly disengaged, as if she was simply going through the motions. And, while a tiny part of her recognised that how she was feeling wasn't normal and was concerned by it, the greatest part of her was too drained to pay any attention. Finn would be back soon anyway, and when he was he could take over, so she could crawl into bed and stay there for a month, at which point maybe they could then talk. In fact, she thought dully as the sound of the front door opening reached her, here he was now.

She felt the air shift, and glanced up from the journal that was sitting open and empty in her lap to find Finn standing in the doorway and emanating a weird sort of taut determination, his face set and his eyes dark.

'Hi,' he said, removing his jacket and rolling the sleeves of his shirt up with an efficient competency that not so long ago would have had her quivering with desire but now left her distressingly unmoved.

'Hi.'

'How have you been?'

Freezing, actually. But spring could be like that. Maybe she ought to have turned the heating on. 'Fine.'

'Why are you sitting in the dark?' He stalked over to a lamp in the corner and switched it on.

'I didn't realise it was so late,' she said, blinking at the sudden light.

'How's Josh?'

'He's fine. He's asleep.' Finally. 'He started crawling yesterday.'

'Did he? I'm sorry I missed that.'

'He's fast,' she said, attempting a weak smile. 'I envy his energy.'

Finn sat down on the ottoman, leaning forwards and resting his elbows on his knees, and peered at her, his eyes narrowing slightly. 'Are you all right?' he asked. 'You look tired.'

'Josh has another tooth coming through. It's been keeping us both up at night.'

'Where's Mrs Gardiner?'

'I gave her a couple of days off.'

His dark brows snapped together. 'Why?'

'It was her granddaughter's birthday. She lives in Wales. Mrs G was keen to go.' And she'd been keen to have her go because even conversation had started being hard work.

'When is she back?'

'I'm not sure.'

'I'll give her a call later.'

'How were your meetings?'

'Fine,' he said, his gaze locking with hers and not letting it go. 'But I don't want to talk about my meetings.'

Of course he didn't. He didn't want to talk to her about anything. Why would he?

'I want to talk about us.'

Oh, the irony. 'There is no us,' she said, her chest nevertheless squeezing.

He went very still, something she couldn't even begin to identify flickering in the depths of his eyes. 'Do you mean that?'

'Yes.'

'Why?'

'Because you clearly don't trust me.'

His eyebrows shot up. 'What?'

'You don't trust me.'

'Why would you think that?'

She closed the journal with a snap, a sudden hot rush of emotion obliterating the numbness and firing her deadened nerve-endings. 'I told you everything about me, Finn. Everything. Yet every time I asked you anything about your parents or anything even vaguely personal you brushed me aside. You told me nothing. Until you absolutely had no choice.'

'What are you talking about?'

'Your adoption. That huge thing that you didn't think to share with me.'

He stared at her, a tiny muscle in his jaw pulsating. 'I couldn't,' he said gruffly. 'I could barely make sense of it myself. I certainly couldn't have talked about it any sooner than I did. With you or anyone.'

'No one else knows?'

'You're the only person I've told. The only person I *wanted* to know, I've recently realised. You unlocked me in that respect. You made me re-evaluate the past and see things from a different perspective. I don't regret any of that. I do, however, regret how that conversation ended. I'm sorry. I let decades-old hang-ups get the better of me. I was an idiot for letting you leave.'

'If you'd told me that I mattered to you and that we were in this together I'd have stayed.'

A flicker of warmth and something that looked like hope leapt in the depths of his eyes. 'You *do* matter to me and we *are* in this together.'

'Because of Josh.'

His gaze intensified and heated. 'Not entirely.'

No, she thought acidly. It wouldn't do to forget the sex side of things, would it? Or to be careless and ignore the need to protect herself. 'Yes, well, I have regrets too.'

'What do you regret?'

'Everything,' she said with deliberate bluntness. 'Our entire relationship is completely wrong.'

He paled. 'In what way?'

'In every way,' she said. 'Would you have chosen to be with me if it wasn't for Josh?'

'That's a wholly unfair question,' he said, his jaw tightening as a flash of wariness flitted across his face. 'Not to mention impossible to answer.'

Which meant no. And only went to prove her point. 'Right from the beginning I've forced you into doing things you can't possibly have wanted to do.'

'Such as?'

'Being a father. Accommodating me and Josh, me in particular. Giving up your evenings. Taking me to bed. The dinner with friends I made you have. Then Paris. The sex. The talking. You name it, I've made you do it.'

He looked at her as though she'd come from another planet. 'That's ridiculous.'

'Is it?'

'Are you serious?'

'Deadly.'

'I have never done anything even remotely reluctantly in my entire life,' he said, his steady gaze fixed to hers. 'If I want to do something, I do it.

If I don't, I don't. If I'd known about Josh sooner I'd have been right there with you every step of the way. The night you came into my room and took off your top I wanted you so badly I was at the end of my tether anyway. I wanted you from the first moment I saw you again. Why do you think I spent so much time out of the apartment when you and Josh first moved in?'

'Work?'

'Not work,' he said darkly. 'I spent every evening in the fitness suite trying to obliterate the need, much good that it did me. If you hadn't come to me that night I would have gone to you. You were just quicker, that's all.' He gave his head a quick shake and then rubbed his hands over his face. 'I didn't deliberately delay us having dinner with friends, although I will admit to wanting you to myself for a while longer. And I didn't need to take you with me to Paris. I've never taken anyone to Paris. Or anywhere else, for that matter. I didn't even need to be there myself. I don't usually. I prefer to stay in the background and let my extremely efficient PR company take care of that side of things.'

She swallowed hard, torn between wanting to believe him and not wanting to believe him. 'So why did you?'

He looked at her for a moment, as if the question had taken him by surprise. 'I wanted to show you my hotel,' he said with a faint smile. 'I wanted to show you off.'

'Not for the sex?'

'We weren't having it then. But I admit there may have been an element of that too. It had been a while.'

'Why didn't you call me?'

'When?'

'At any point over the last forty-eight hours. It occurred to me that you might be busy thinking about your other family.'

'I wasn't. I spent the hours I wasn't in meetings processing the grief for my father that was interrupted when I found that certificate. And then thinking about what you said, how right you were and trying to figure it all out in my head. Would you have answered if I had called?'

'Possibly not,' she had to admit.

He leaned forwards and peered at her closely, confusion swirling in the depths of his eyes, a deep frown creasing his forehead. 'What's going on, Georgie? Where is all this coming from?'

Wasn't it obvious? It was all coming from him. From their situation. From his lack of trust and her crushing disappointment that he wasn't the man she'd desperately wanted him to be. From the realisation that they had no relationship outside parenting Josh and never would. From his shattering of her heart and the subsequent fracturing of her dreams.

Or was it?

Finn was still staring at her, his gaze clear and unwavering, as if he was trying to see into her soul, his presence about the only solid thing she could fix on. And through the fog of nothingness in her head, there was a spark of…something.

Light.

Clarity.

A seed of doubt planted itself in her head, its roots spreading fast and wide. That tiny voice of concern grew louder. And as fragments of what Finn had been saying spun through her thoughts, solidifying, gaining credence, gaining volume, those doubts exploded and she went icy cold.

Oh, God.

What if all this had come not from him but from *her*? From her insecurities, from her illness? What if this was the setback, possibly even the depression, she'd been fearing?

As she frantically analysed everything that had happened over the last couple of days, the way she'd been feeling, the suspiciousness, the hopelessness and the sadness, her heart began to race and a cold sweat broke out all over her skin.

She was right in the middle of it, she realised with a sickening jolt. One tug of the rug from beneath her feet, one toss of the sea and she'd tumbled into a return of the paranoia, a deadening lack of energy, of libido, and icy numbness.

That was all it had taken.

She wasn't better, she thought as a shaft of agony and despair cut through her and she began to tremble all over. She wasn't anywhere near better. She may never be. And it was crucifying.

'I'm sorry, I can't do this,' she said, her throat tight and her eyes stinging.

'Can't do what?'

'Whatever it is you think we're doing.'

His dark gaze didn't leave hers, but it did nothing to calm the distress suddenly whirling around inside her. 'I think we're building a relationship,' he said. 'A real relationship.'

'We aren't,' she said hoarsely. Even if he *was* the man she'd thought he was—and God, she didn't know which version to believe any more—they couldn't be. She wasn't capable of it. She wasn't strong enough. She didn't know if she ever would be. 'We never have been.'

'I disagree. Our civil partnership stopped being a pragmatic arrangement weeks ago. If it ever was in the first place.' He stopped and took a deep breath. 'I love you, Georgie.'

As the words hit her brain a bolt of panic shot through her, denial screaming at her. 'No.'

'Yes,' he said, his eyes suddenly blazing with a heat that only emphasised how cold and confused she felt. 'I am head over heels in love with you.'

How could he be when even she didn't know who she was anymore? 'You don't know me.'

'I do. I know exactly who you are. And I think you love me too.'

That was what she'd thought once too but now she didn't know what to think. 'I don't know you.'

'You know me better than anyone.'

'Even if I could believe that, even if you're right, I can't be what you want,' she said, her voice breaking. How could she possibly lumber him with her when she was like this? How fair on him would it be if she had a setback every time he did or said something unexpected? How long would it be before they were both walking on eggshells, communicating only about their son?

'Yes, you can. You already are.'

'Do you want more children?'

'Not if you don't.'

'I don't believe you.'

'OK, maybe I would like Josh to have siblings,' he said. 'Maybe I would like to be part of a bigger family. But there's surrogacy. Or, dare I say it, adoption?'

He'd already thought that far ahead? 'I'm sorry,' she said, growing cold with fear and desperation. 'I can't handle this right now. It's all too much.'

'Either way, Georgie, I'm not letting you go. I told you I'd keep you safe and I meant it. Whatever is going on we'll deal with it together.'

'No. We can't.'

'We can.'

'You don't understand.'

'I'm trying to.'

'It's impossible.'

'Nothing is impossible.'

This is, she thought, sadness and confusion pouring through her. *This is*.

'I need to go.'

He recoiled as if she'd slapped him. 'Where?'

'I don't know,' she said, scrambling to her feet and taking a shaky step back. 'Somewhere else.'

'Don't fight me,' he said, his voice cracking as he rose too. 'Fight *for* me. Like I'm trying to fight for you. For us.'

'I told you before, there is no us.'

'You don't mean that.'

'I do.'

'I've never begged for anything,' he said, his voice low and rough, 'but I'm begging you. If you won't stay for me, at least stay for our son.'

Why? What was the point? What good could she possibly be to anyone while still so ill? 'He'll be far better off with you than me.'

'He needs *you*. *I* need you. I love you.' He raked his hands through his hair, his eyes wild with confusion and desperation. 'Georgie, you matter so much to me. The night we met I felt we had a connection that went far beyond chemistry. It was like something in me instinctively recognised something in you. And it's only grown since then. Everything about you fascinates me. The way you twist your hair and chew on your pen. The way you are with our son, your patience and your gentleness. You're the strongest, most incredible person I've ever met. You confront your fears and deal with them and you've made me do that too. You let me get away with nothing. You're beautiful and clever and funny and the woman I love. I've never felt like this about anyone ever. I don't want to be without you, Georgie. I can't.'

'I'm sorry,' she said, her eyes stinging and her throat tight as she stumbled back in the direction of the door.

'Don't do this. Please.'

'I have to.'

He moved towards her and put his hands on her shoulders, his expression fierce. 'You don't.'

'I do,' she cried, wrenching away.

'Where will you go?'

'I'll let you know.'

'It's late.'

'I'll be fine.'

'I won't let you do this, Georgie. I won't let you leave. Not this time.'

'This time,' she said, turning and heading for the door before the tears could spill over, 'you don't have any choice.'

CHAPTER THIRTEEN

As THE DOOR closing rang in his ears, Finn stood there rooted to the spot, reeling as torment and bewilderment spun through him.

What the hell had just happened?

He'd returned home, all fired up with ferocious determination and the hammering need to put things right, the rings he'd bought her in Paris burning a hole in his pocket. He didn't know what he'd expected to find on his arrival. He hadn't given it much thought. However, if he had, Georgie sitting on the sofa in the dark, pale and drawn, would not have been it. The sight of her had knocked him for six. Concern had slammed into him. But nothing had stunned him as much as the conversation that had then ensued.

He felt as if he'd stepped into an alternative universe, one in which there were no rules and nothing made sense. Did she really believe everything she'd said? he wondered, his head spinning and his gut churning. That they had no relationship and never would? How could she, after everything they'd been through together?

Yet that was how it seemed. The more he'd tried to convince her that they did have something, that he loved her, the more she'd backed off. It had been like trying to hold on to water and somehow, unintentionally and agonisingly, he'd made things worse.

Georgie was not in a good way—she'd walked out on *their son*—and his entire body began to ache with the knowledge that perhaps he couldn't help her. Perhaps he'd never be able to help her. Her despair, her desperation and the tears that she'd struggled to contain cut through him like a knife. He'd thought he could bind her to him with a civil partnership, but no ties were strong enough to overcome this. Nor was how he felt about her, because he'd tried everything. He'd tried reasoning with her and then pleaded with her and it had made no difference. He didn't know how to fix this. Never had he felt so powerless. It was agony. It was terrifying.

But there was one thing he did know. When she'd told him he didn't have a choice she'd been wrong. Dead wrong. It was pretty much the only thing he did have right now, and, despite not having a clue about anything, he was making it because he was *not* losing her again.

Georgie fled down the hall, the tears that she'd been wretchedly holding back spilling over and streaking down her cheeks. With every step she took the knife slicing her heart to pieces struck harder and faster, the pain flowing through her veins unbearable.

Why was this happening to her? she thought with a desperate sniff. Why was life, her illness, so cruel? What had she ever done to deserve any of it? Why couldn't she be happy? Why couldn't she be normal?

Reaching the lift, she pressed the button with one trembling finger, but the lift seemed to be as broken as she was because nothing happened, no matter how much she jabbed away at it. And she really needed it to work because she had to escape. She had to find somewhere to hole up and lick her wounds, wounds that were raw and deep and indelible.

But what if there was no escape? a little voice inside her head cried. What if no matter how far she ran, how hard she tried, this was always going to be her reality? What if she was destined to be dogged by what had happened for the rest of her life, never happy, never normal? She couldn't run for ever. She didn't want to be that person, constantly in fear of the present and the future, continually up and down, vulnerable and helpless. She *wasn't* that person. She wouldn't be. She had to face up to it.

Starting now.

What was she doing? she asked herself urgently, taking a step back from the lift, away from the edge. Where was she planning on heading? Was she *really* going to walk away from Josh? From Finn? Who claimed to love her? Who maybe *did* love her?

In the still quiet of the hall, the only sound in her ears the hammering of her heart, Georgie thought about the calm, steadfast way he'd countered all her accusations. About his strength and resilience in the face of her increasing panic. About everything he'd said and done over the last few months. If she accepted that she'd been in the grip of paranoia and doubt caused by her illness then she also had to accept that his version of events was the right one.

And God, she wanted it to be. She had to take a chance on them. She *wanted* to take a chance on them. Because she loved him back. He *was* the man she'd imagined him to be. She hadn't got that wrong. The happiness she'd felt hadn't been an illusion. Nor had any of the feelings she had before she'd left Paris. Everything had been real. Her hopes and dreams still lay within her grasp if only she was brave enough to grab them.

She would take control of this thing winding its wicked tendrils around her thoughts and emotions, she promised herself as she blew her nose and set her jaw. Come hell or high water, she *would* beat it. She'd seek help and go back on the medication. She should never have stopped taking it in the first place. What had she been thinking when she'd even been warned of the dangers of doing exactly that? She was going to fight for herself. And fight for Finn, for them, just as he'd asked her to.

With determination powering through her, Georgie spun on her heel and retraced her steps, only to slam to a halt a moment later at the sight of Finn striding down the hall towards her.

'This is not happening,' he said with a fierceness on his handsome face that heated all the places that had been so cold lately. 'You are not leaving me. You are not leaving Josh. I love you and you don't get to run away. I won't allow it. I know it's complicated but we'll figure it out. Together.'

'Yes,' she said simply, the emotion pummelling her on the inside practically wiping out her knees. There was much, *much* more that she wanted to say but her throat was so tight and the emotion so thick that she couldn't. All she could do was throw her arms around his neck and pull his head down to hers and kiss him with everything she was feeling.

With a harsh groan Finn whipped one arm around her waist and the other around her shoulders, pulling her tightly against him as he kissed her back with equal heat and need and desperation.

'God, Georgie,' he muttered when he eventually lifted his head, his breath ragged, his heart pounding against hers.

'I'm so sorry,' she said, hearing the catch in her voice and swallowing hard. 'I had a relapse and panicked. I convinced myself that you weren't who I thought you were. I've been so confused. So lost.'

'So have I,' he said passionately. 'But we belong together. We belong to each other.'

'I don't want to live without Josh. Or you. I love you.'

He rested his forehead against hers and she could feel him shaking with emotion. 'I think I fell in love with you the moment you walked up to me in my club and asked me if you could join me. You were dazzling.'

'I'm not that person any longer.'

'You're all that and more.'

'I still need help.'

'We'll get it,' he said, stroking his thumbs over her cheeks to smooth away the tracks of her tears and the remnants of her fears. 'I will always be there for you, Georgie, whatever happens.'

'And I'll always be there for you.'

He kissed her again, this time more gently, more deeply, and by the time he lifted his head, the sense of peace and hope and joy that had been beginning to spin through her filled her to the brim, overwhelming her all over again.

'Don't cry,' he said, kissing away the tears. 'It'll be all right.'

'Will it?'

'Of course,' he said gruffly. 'I bought you these,' he added, digging his hand briefly into his pocket and then sliding a plain gold band and then a stunning diamond solitaire onto the third finger of her left hand. 'In Paris.'

'They're beautiful,' she said, her throat tightening and her heart swelling as she placed her hand over his heart and looked at them.

'You're beautiful.'

'I'm a mess.'

'You're mine.'

'Your lift is broken,' she said with a watery sniff.

'I had it stopped.'

'You had it stopped?'

'I couldn't risk losing you again,' he said, his eyes darkening with emotion, his hold on her strong and secure.

'You won't.'

'Promise?'

She nodded. 'I promise.'

EPILOGUE

Ospedale San Giovanni,
Venice

PROPPED UP IN bed in the dark, quiet private hospital room where his shattered body was gradually healing, Federico Rossi stared one last time at the image on the screen, a photo of a couple at the recent launch of the seven-star Hotel Bellevue in Paris—at one Finn Calvert in particular, a man who was the spitting image of himself but without the scars and the broken nose—and slowly, thoughtfully, closed the lid of his laptop.

* * * * *

Wrapped up in the drama of
The Secrets She Must Tell?
You'll love the next installment in the
Lost Sons of Argentina trilogy!

And why not lose yourself in these
other Lucy King stories?

The Reunion Lie
The Best Man for the Job
The Party Starts at Midnight
A Scandal Made in London

Available now

WE HOPE YOU ENJOYED
THIS BOOK FROM
⟨H⟩ HARLEQUIN
PRESENTS

Escape to exotic locations where passion knows no bounds.

Welcome to the glamorous lives of royals and billionaires, where passion knows no bounds. Be swept into a world of luxury, wealth and exotic locations.

8 NEW BOOKS AVAILABLE EVERY MONTH!

#3885 AFTER THE BILLIONAIRE'S WEDDING VOWS...
by Lucy Monroe

Greek tycoon Andros's whirlwind romance with Polly started white-hot. Five years later, the walls he's built threaten to push her away forever! With his marriage on the line, Andros must win back his wife. Their passion still burns bright, but can it break down their barriers?

#3886 FORBIDDEN HAWAIIAN NIGHTS
Secrets of the Stowe Family
by Cathy Williams

Max Stowe is commanding and completely off-limits as Mia Kaiwi's temporary boss! But there's no escape from temptation working so closely together... Dare she explore their connection for a few scorching nights?

#3887 THE PLAYBOY PRINCE OF SCANDAL
The Acostas!
by Susan Stephens

Prince Cesar will never forgive polo star Sofia Acosta for the article branding him a playboy! But to avoid further scandal he must invite her to his lavish banquet in Rome. Where he's confronted by her unexpected apology and their *very* obvious electricity!

#3888 THE MAN SHE SHOULD HAVE MARRIED
by Louise Fuller

Famed movie director Farlan has come a long way from the penniless boy whose ring Nia rejected. But their surprise reunion proves there's one thing he'll never be able to relinquish...their dangerously electric connection!

YOU CAN FIND MORE INFORMATION ON UPCOMING HARLEQUIN TITLES, FREE EXCERPTS AND MORE AT HARLEQUIN.COM.

HPCNMRB0121

"Mr. Alexandris," Tansy pronounced rather stiffly.

"Come sit down," he invited lazily. "Tea or coffee?"

"Coffee please," Tansy said, following him around a sectional room
divider into a rather more intimate space furnished with sumptuous
sofas and then sinking down into the comfortable depths of one, her
tense spine rigorously protesting that amount of relaxation.

She was fighting to get a grip on her composure again but nothing
about Jude Alexandris in the flesh matched the formal online images
she had viewed. He wasn't wearing a sharply cut business suit—he
was wearing faded, ripped and worn jeans that outlined long, powerful
thighs and narrow hips and accentuated the prowling natural grace
of his every movement. An equally casual dark gray cotton top
complemented the jeans. One sleeve was partially pushed up to reveal
a strong brown forearm and a small tattoo that appeared to be printed
letters of some sort. His garb reminded her that although he might be
older than her, he was still only in his late twenties, and that unlike her,
he had felt no need to dress to impress.

Her pride stung at the knowledge that she was little more than a
commodity on Alexandris's terms. Either he would choose her or he
wouldn't. She had put herself on the market to be bought, though,
she thought with sudden self-loathing. How could she blame Jude
Alexandris for her stepfather's use of virtual blackmail to get her
agreement? Everything she was doing was for Posy, she reminded
herself squarely, and the end would justify the means...wouldn't it?

"So..." Tansy remarked in a stilted tone because she was
determined not to sit there acting like the powerless person she knew
herself to be in his presence. "You require a fake wife..."

Jude shifted a broad shoulder in a very slight shrug. "Only we would know it was fake. It would have to seem real to everyone else from the start to the very end," he advanced calmly. "Everything between us would have to remain confidential."

"I'm not a gossip, Mr. Alexandris." In fact, Tansy almost laughed at the idea of even having anyone close enough to confide in, because she had left her friends behind at university, and certainly none of them had seemed to understand her decision to make herself responsible for her baby sister rather than return to the freedom of student life.

"I trust no one," Jude countered without apology. "You would be legally required to sign a nondisclosure agreement before I married you."

"Understood. My stepfather explained that to me," Tansy acknowledged, her attention reluctantly drawn to his careless sprawl on the sofa opposite, the long, muscular line of a masculine thigh straining against well-washed denim. Her head tipped back, her color rising as she made herself look at his face instead, encountering glittering dark eyes that made the breath hitch in her throat.

"I find you attractive, too," Jude Alexandris murmured as though she had spoken.

"I don't know what you're talking about," Tansy protested, the faint pink in her cheeks heating exponentially. Her stomach flipped while she wondered if she truly could be read that easily by a man.

"For this to work, we would need that physical attraction. Nobody is likely to be fooled by two strangers pretending what they don't feel, least of all my family, some of whom are shrewd judges of character."

Tansy had paled. "Why would we need attraction? I assumed this was to be a marriage on paper, nothing more."

"Then you assumed wrong," Jude told her without skipping a beat.

Don't miss
The Greek's Convenient Cinderella
*available February 2021 wherever
Harlequin Presents books and ebooks are sold.*

Harlequin.com

Get 4 FREE REWARDS!

We'll send you 2 FREE Books plus 2 FREE Mystery Gifts.

PRESENTS

Cinderella in the Sicilian's World
SHARON KENDRICK

PRESENTS

Proof of Their Forbidden Night
CHANTELLE SHAW

Harlequin Presents books feature the glamorous lives of royals and billionaires in a world of exotic locations, where passion knows no bounds.

FREE
Value Over
$20